**I bet my boss is worse than yours.**

**Does yours make you run laps, clean up monster spit, or stand guard at the world's most boring City Council event ever?**

Yeah. Welcome to the Tres Lunas Police and Investigation Academy. Hooray for me. Why did I join again? Because I'm a wingless part-fairy looking for validation? No. Shut up.

I'm a bad mofo. That's why I joined.

And that's why I'm constantly avoiding the chief. He's a dragon shifter who's got the hots for me. But I don't dip my toes in the company pool, no matter how tempting the skinny dipping might be.

Then, there's this murder. On live TV. At the event I'm guarding.

Really, can my life get any worse?

It can when the murderer is a serial killer ...

FML.

# Shift Happens

Fae'd Up and Frustrated - Book 2

# ANNA DARE

Le Rue Publishing
320 South Boston Avenue, Suite 1030
Tulsa, OK 74103
www.LeRuePublishing.com

ISBN: 978-0-9985437-9-6

*To S. for being a good sport.*

*And Cass for her birthday.*

Ever met a sadist? Like a true, honest-to-God torturer? Join the Tres Lunas Police and Investigation Academy, because apparently that's where evil people work.

And apparently, I was stupid enough to sign up. Which is why I'm here, under the eye of a sadist, doing push-ups, just like I have every night for the past month. At the freaking crack of sunset.

Yup. My hometown isn't just a haven for magical creatures in So. Cal. It's apparently a place for enchanted torment.

Damn! That sounds like a dirty strip-club name. Enchanted Torment … better not tell Tabby that. I can just see my friend, a tiny seventy-year-old crystal-ball wielding peeper, throwing her life savings into a club like that. Complete with male were-animal strippers … I imagine Tabby, my elderly neighbor Mrs. Snow, and their bunco group howling and dancing near the stage.

I have to suck down a laugh and hold it in my aching lungs.

Eff. My wandering brain has stopped my muscles and paused my arms. And the boss has noticed. Lyon Fox, get it together!

I glare at Diego Flores, the overly buff commander who is currently eying my stalled push-ups with a lip curled in disgust.

Uncurl that lip, Mr. Flores. These biceps weren't trained from the age of three to embrace pain like yours.

I hate Diego (whose nickname by the way, is ironically, Flowers) with a passion that rivals my hatred for all things spicy. I list spicy things as I shake through the last few push-ups of the night.

Cumin, better than Flowers.

Tabasco, nicer than Flowers.

Ghost peppers, as evil as Flowers.

Done. Finally.

I fall to the mat, not even caring that it's been the site of many a sweaty man's nethers during our wrestling matches.

My blonde hair splays out and I close my baby blues, cursing myself for thinking that becoming an investigator was a good idea. My breath saws jaggedly in and out as I ask myself why I chose this over being a paralegal.

Because I'm dumb. Clearly.

It's just five more months. Just five more months … I don't think five months has felt this long since I was a kid. And it's only five months of half nights of sweaty hellscape exercise.

I'll live. Probably.

Right now, I spend five hours a night at the Academy and five more at the office training on paperwork. I'm a month in. Just five to go. Unfortunately, the workout is the first two hours every night at the Academy.

I open my eyes to peek at the clock on the wall of the gym. We haven't hit the two-hour mark tonight. Gah!

Flowers—I seriously think he must have some demon blood in there somewhere, though officially he's a tiger-shifter—leans over me and whispers, "One more, Fox."

No! No more. But there is no arguing with the brown-eyed, cut-jawed severity of Flowers. He gives orders and we follow.

My arms tremble like baby deer legs as I force my body into position. I hiss through my teeth. "I hate you." But I do it.

One more shaky up and down that burns all the way from the tips of my fingers to the tips of my toes.

"Way to push through." He slaps me on the butt with the flick of his towel before moving off to torture someone else.

I collapse for the second time and the room goes hazy for a second. Perhaps I've died. If he's killed me, I'm totally going ghost and haunting his toned abs. Literally. I think I'll pop my head through his stomach and start talking at strategic moments. I smile as I picture ruining every date he'll ever have.

Seena and Becca, two other Academy recruits, reach down and grab my hands. Together, they use all their strength to haul my noodle limbs up so we can go jump over some tires.

You know, because I see the police doing that every day. Job essential. Obviously.

I've tried to bring up my theory that if we want real-world skills we should practice napping in cars, but Flowers didn't appreciate my insight.

"Come on, let's get this over with," Becca says under her breath before giving me a tiny grin that shows a hint of dimple. Then she adjusts her brunette ponytail, even though there isn't a hair out of place. I find it ridiculously unfair that she's adorable even when sweaty. I probably look like something the cat dragged in and puked on.

Flowers separates the recruits out so we're three across on one side of the gym, facing a line of ten tires laid across our blue workout mats. Huge, smelly, black tires.

Our lovely boss blows a whistle like it's kindergarten gym class. "When the person in front of you is three tires ahead, you start. First row. Go!" Flowers adds a hand clap because the whistle wasn't enough in his opinion.

I'm toward the back, so I get a breather. Thank goodness.

Seena is in the line right next to me and I glance over at him with "save me" puppy dog eyes. He mirrors my expression, though his black hair is plastered to his forehead and a drop of sweat dripping into his eye ruins the effect a bit. The dude's a Persian shifter who's new to town. Haven't asked him what kind of shifter yet because we haven't quite made it past complaints about this job, our last job, exes. There's just so much to complain about in a person's life. We've really bonded over our hatreds, particularly of the first two hours of the evening.

Actually, I do know a thing or two. Seena's in this thing because he's some kind of genius analyst who wants a legal reason to hack computers and outsmart other nerds. And apparently he got bored over at LAPD because—and I quote — "Humans just don't know how to be as devious. We've had centuries more practice."

He thinks working as an investigator in Tres Lunas will be more interesting than his last job. Only problem? Every investigator is required to go through the Academy.

"Damn initiation rituals," Seena moans as he rubs his shoulder and I try not to notice the sweat stains on his pits. (Yuck.)

I envy my buddy's ability to curse this moment aloud. Wish I could. My fairy mother thought cursing was a nasty habit of mine when I was a teenager. So, what'd she do? Hired a witch to curse me with a cursing curse. Meaning I can't cuss when I stub my toe or hate my boss. My tongue won't do it. Ever.

I try to make up for it internally. But that's not really the same. The best I can do is spit out some texty abbreviated curses, or some lamebrain options like—

"It's total horse puckey." I nod fervently, agreeing with Seena.

Becca moves forward in the line on my other side and grins. "That's a cute one." She's an effervescent and cheerful sprite, whom I befriended against all odds. Normally, I don't like girls as bubbly as soda pop. And I definitely don't like my curses being called cute.

But there's something about Becca that's just so damn lovable. Maybe it's the fact that she's got one of those perfect heart-shaped faces with eternally pinchable cheeks.

"The fun team is ready to rock!" She crosses her eyes and does a devil sign with her hands.

*Screech!* That would be the whistle that Flowers clearly purchased from a demon for the sole purpose of turning recruits deaf.

Our turn.

Yippee.

We go.

Not gracefully or grandly. We. Just. Go.

Achingly. Haltingly. A bit clumsily.

Seena puffs as he runs the tires next to me, pulling his knees up way higher than necessary. Overachiever. "Okay. You ready? Persian insult … of the day: zahré mar. It means … poison of the snake. Like bullshit—"

"How are those even … equivalent?" Becca asks from my other side, her words punctuated by hard breathing. "I mean … bullshit stinks. Gross. But snake poison? Not … the same level. Death. Totally illogical."

"They both suck … to step on?" Seena offers. "I don't decide translations. I'm just here … to expand your vocab."

"Well, that translation's … zahré mar," Becca retorts.

"Too busy dying … to learn! … Zahré mar!" I retort, as my legs catch on fire. Seena's been on this kick to help me

7

expand my cursing abilities. Apparently, my mom's curse doesn't pick up on Persian words.

"Good!" Seena pants. "Both proper uses."

"Whoop!" Becca loses her balance next to me and careens sideways. Her hand flies out and latches onto my arm. I trip, spinning as I tumble and somehow falling face first into Seena's back. His spine does its best to crack my nose as he trips over the tire he's in and crashes into the cadet in front of him, and we create a domino effect, effectively felling those in front of us.

*Screech!*

Flowers blows on his whistle.

Dazed, I sit up, clutching my poor nose, rubbing at the jewel embedded in my chin, and just basically checking all my aching parts are still there.

In a demonstration of how caring and compassionate he is, Flowers snaps, "Okay dimwits. Since tires are too complicated, let's do laps."

His glare at our trio clearly spells out who's responsible for the laps. Thanks, man. As if this hazing thing wasn't enough. Like tripping was Becca's fault? She's barely five feet! Those tires are almost as high as her knees.

We groan, detangle, and run laps. And laps. And laps.

Until we finally hit that blessed two-hour mark.

But we don't get to collapse as our lungs rightfully want to do. Nope. Shower? Nope. Those pores can keep on leaking.

We get to move on to practicing spells.

I groan.

Spells are not my thing. I'm a mutt. My mom has some strange amalgamation of fairy blood—white, fall, flower... you name it, it's in her gene pool. It's been diluted over the centuries by other creatures and humans too. My dad? Full human. So, though I'm fairy enough to have been born with a blue jewel in my chin and black toenails, magic ain't my game, yo. That's my fairy gangster voice. It's what I used to use whenever I was pretending to be standoffish when I'd visit my mother beyond the Veil. It totally worked. Made all the powerful fairies back right off. Yeah. I wish.

I do have two minuscule powers. The first is—you guessed it (because every magical creature's got it)—quick healing. Maybe I'd feel better about this one if I was a were-animal and prone to fights for alpha status. Or if I was a troll who just liked to fight. But I'm basically a reading-and-junk-food-obsessed shut in. So that power's never been all that good to me. (I've totally suppressed the memories of the time I was attacked by a crazy vampire and later accused of her murder. So not bringing it up.)

My other lamebrain power is ... wait for it. Losing things. Yup. That's me. Need something lost? I can do it for you.

Flowers is under some delusion that I can learn to enhance my power. Ha. Yeah. I can see that being so useful as an investigator. Let me help you lose your keys. No keys? How about your kid?

I rub a tired hand over my face and try to ignore how every part of me is throbbing and begging for water. I need to tamp the sarcasm down and focus. Otherwise, I'm not gonna make any 'progress' and I'll be on Flower's shit list.

The bottom three recruits each night get tasked with some awful assignment. And he's clearly gunning for my little trio since we caused the pileup, even though that was a completely and totally coulda-happened-to-anybody mistake.

Unfair.

But Flowers has never claimed that fairness is his middle name.

I line up near Becca and grab a couple of gray foam yoga blocks. I'm supposed to try to 'lose them' to a specific location.

I stare at my block, which is missing a tiny chunk in one corner. I concentrate. Visualize. Like all the self-help spell books say to do. "I've lost my yoga block in the men's locker room." The block disappears, fading from my hands in a blink.

But does it go to the men's locker room? Of course not. Instead, it reappears just above Flowers head. It hovers there just long enough for me to spot it, for my mouth to drop open in amused horror. And then—

*Bonk.*

My classmates all laugh. I can't help it. I laugh. He didn't even see it coming.

But I stop laughing when he marches right over to me. The pupil of his eyes thins and a glint of his tiger glimmers in his glare.

"Fox!"

"Yessir." My muscles are clenching on instinct, trying to curl inward and protect themselves.

"I'm going to assume that was a mistake." He steps in close, showcasing how much bigger he is.

"Yes, sir, it was." My voice doesn't squeak. No, that's just my ears malfunctioning.

"Please demonstrate your spell."

I try not to let my hands shake as Flowers death-stares me all while staying inside my personal space bubble. Seriously, I don't know where he learned to glare like that, but it's got all the intensity of a death ray. I'm ready to cry and run at the same time.

Not to mention the fact that every eye in the gym is now about to watch me showcase my lame powers. Hooray. I'd hoped to fly under the radar through the Academy. No such luck.

I grab a new block. I stare at the gray cube, willing it to behave.

"I've lost my yoga block in the men's locker room."

*Bonk.*

This time the block appears a few feet away and bonks Seena on the head.

"Hey!" Seena throws the block at me and misses.

Flowers's lips don't even twitch. I wonder if he's secretly a cyborg.

"You're not focusing." He grabs another block from my pile and steps closer, until we're toe to toe and I'm pretty sure I'm inhaling his exhales. Ew.

He shoves another new block into my hands.

Right now, all I can focus on is holding my breath and attempting not to crack under his steely-eyed glare. Because Academy isn't for the weak. The weak get cut, or so Flowers says.

My BFF might think he was sexy. She might love this moment. JR's got a thing for strong Latino men. But Flowers is frickin' intense. In a scary way.

I turn my head slowly and take a calming, cautious sip of un-Flowers-tainted air. Don't tempt the monster, Lyon. Don't do it.

"Stop trying to be a clown. Send that block somewhere serious."

"Like your office? That's about the most serious room in the building." Dammit! That just slipped out. My sense of self-preservation sucks.

A middle-school-like chorus of "Oooooooh," sounds off around us.

I fight the urge to give him a cocky grin.

Nope.

Don't do it.

Don't get fired.

A deep breath. That's his only reaction. A deep breath. This guy's got nerves of titanium. I can't help but admire that a little. Until he leans in, face an inch away, eyes full-on tiger.

I'm scared again. My sphincter is clenching like it's never clenched before.

Flowers speaks slowly and clearly, his hot breath fogging up my unblinking eyes. "Fill my office with blocks, Fox. Until you do, you've earned a permanent spot on my list."

Mother eff. Frickin' idiot. I'm so stupid. Mayor of the Dummies. Captain of the Cockleheaded.

Flowers straightens and his nostrils flare for a second as he eyes me. Then he saunters off, all cool confidence.

I drop my block and ball my free hands into fists to keep myself from throwing the block at him. Seriously, my inner-three-year-old wants to resist and riot in this no-win situation.

Once Flowers is long gone and occupied with someone else, Seena comes over and pats me on the head. "Don't worry, Lyon. I'm sure a spot on the list will only be the worst thing possible short of death." His massive, straight eyelash-fringed brown eyes glitter with amusement.

I want to yank out some of those unfairly long eyelashes, but I settle for smacking him in the stomach.

Seena takes it like a computer nerd and crumples to the floor. I feel slightly better for being mean. Pecking order right? Until he winks up at me and hops to his feet. Dammit! Faker!

Can nothing go my way tonight?

Becca bumps my shoulder from the other side. Well, a little lower than my shoulder because she's so darn short. I glance over to see if she's sympathizing over the Seena thing but her eyes are not on me. She's staring across the massive gymnasium. "Meow. Who's that?" She not-so-subtly jerks her head toward the double doors, where a man has just stepped inside.

Panic.

Neon green, blinking flashing panic.

"Frick. Frick. Frick." I pull her in front of me and try to hide, forgetting that she's too short because all my logic is not logic-ing. Inside my head, the little men who run the show have abandoned their posts. There are fires. Sirens. Riots. It's chaos.

"What's wrong?" Becca asks.

"That's the double ex," Seena whispers across me as I shift gears and pull him closer, trying to use the two of them as human shields.

"Is that a porn reference? God, I hope he's on film naked somewhere," Becca giggles as the figure starts to swagger forward.

I smack the back of her arm. "No. That's my ex."

"What's double ex mean then?"

Seena raises an eyebrow as Bennett spots me and veers in our direction, his confident walk making the other recruits part like water. My new buddy betrays me and says, "It means Ly-Ly was stupid enough to break up with this guy twice."

"No!" Becca turns to me. "Say it isn't true?"

I duck further behind Seena, not giving up the ruse, though Bennett's eyes are locked on mine when I peek out from the gap between Seena's side and his elbow.

Black hair, piercing green eyes, chiseled jaw. A full-on dragon-shifter heartthrob. That I told I needed a break.

Because... I stare at his eyes. He's gazing back so intensely that my heart skips. I have a hard time remembering why we're on a break.

Becca moves behind Seena and catches me with a dopey expression. She smacks me. "You broke up with that?"

Her hit snaps me out of the spell his eyes have put on me.

"Yup."

My eyes slip to Bennett's pecs, outlined in detail by the wife-beater he's wearing. He's also got on official Tres Lunas Investigation sweats which are doing *everything* good for him.

He must be here for a workout. My mind slips back to the workouts he used to give me in the bedroom. And suddenly,

I'm sweating for a reason that has nothing to do with my aching muscles.

"Are you crazy?" Becca stage whispers.

"Maybe," I reply. Right now my insides are as tangled as a wind chime after a storm.

Bennett reaches us and stops two feet away. He gives respectful nods to greet Seena and Becca. And then he leans sideways to catch my eye again.

"Ms. Fox. Can I have a word?"

Shit. He's sought me out and is being formal. This can't be good.

2

**B**ennett steers me over to a shadowy corner of the room away from everyone else. I clutch a yoga block as my new shield since Becca and Seena eagerly abandoned me to my fate. Dammit.

I wish JR was here to run interference. Best friends should be required to be surgically attached to your hip. That should be a law.

"It's been a month," Bennett states flatly. No small talk. He just jumps right into the argument, skipping the intro paragraph, the topic sentence. His English teacher would be disappointed.

"Okay," I hedge.

"It's been long enough to prove that you got this job without me."

I close my eyes and disappointment plops down in my stomach like a sharp, heavy stone.

He doesn't get it.

And *that's* the problem. Has been a problem ever since I got "promoted" from paralegal to the District Attorney's investigation team. Where Bennett is the head of Felony Investigations. My boss.

"I'm still in the Academy. Still training. And haven't proven myself on a case yet." There are still eighteen thousand ways people can look at me and think: yeah, she doesn't got it. Or…I know exactly how she got here.

I'm not the world's best recruit. I might even be the joke of the department. But like hell if I want to be the punchline for that quip.

Bennett carefully controls his response since curious eyes are darting our way. But that amazing jaw of his twitches. For a second, I imagine making it twitch under much more pleasant circumstances and a tiny bit of longing thumb-wrestles with my disappointment. But it can't win. Rock smashes thumb and scissors and all that.

"You solved Georgina's murder."

I jerk my head toward the class behind me. "That's not what they'll think. Solving it because the murderer shows up at your apartment to kill you too? Yeah, great solve. I didn't even leave his name on the voicemail to you before I got inside. Nobody will believe that."

His fists clench.

"Why do you care so much what other people think?"

"Why don't you?"

"Because I just spent two damn years fighting for the right to be with you and I want to be with you."

My knees tremble. I'm not sure if it's from Bennett's swoon-worthy statement or all the laps. But his words affect me. He went rogue for me. Rejected his dragon clan. I know he's done a lot. I almost reach out to push his hair back, trace his jaw, stare into those emerald eyes. But I stop myself.

"Ben, I want their respect."

"More than you want to be with me."

"You don't understand. You're the boss. You have years of experience backing you up."

He takes a step closer and growls next to my ear.

"I understand that you're torturing me. Look at you in that tight white t-shirt that's soaked through—"

"With sweat. Because I'm working."

"It's practically see through. And they're all staring at you."

I sigh. "Not a single cadet has hit on me. They're only staring right now because they're wondering why the idiot who got on Flower's *list* is getting a talking to from the boss."

"I can get you off that list."

"Don't you dare!" This time I growl. "No special treatment. We agreed."

He lifts an eyebrow. "Maybe I'll give you special treatment until you agree to go out with me. Then you won't have any excuse not to."

"You'd make my life a living H-E-double hockey sticks."

"Is that what it takes, Ly?"

Fury pulses through my veins. I can't believe he's threatening this. "If you do that, I will *never* date you."

"Then what? How long?"

"I don't know, okay? I need to get through Academy, get an assignment..."

Bennett runs a hand over his face. "You want me to wait half a year?" His growl is strained. "That's not a break, Ly. That's breaking up."

With that, he strides out, smacking the gym doors open so hard they hit the walls.

AFTER THAT, MY NIGHT GOES TO SHIT. MY SPELLS DON'T work. I'm listless through our lectures. Showering and changing for the office doesn't snap me out of it.

I'm glazed over at my desk at the Investigation Office where I'm supposed to study closed case files. All I want is to curl up in a ball with a giant bag of jellybeans and let oblivion take over. I wish I could call Jacob, my pseudo-father figure, but he's still visiting friends. Last time he called to check in, he was at a reservation in New Mexico. Howling it up with some coyote-shifter pals.

I do text JR under my desk, but I can't go into details at the office. Can't break down in front of Seena and Becca, who are currently eyeing me cautiously from our adjoined cubicles, like I'm a bomb about to explode. Which I kinda am.

*Bennett is back to blacklist.*

*What'd butthead do?*

*Broke up for real.*

*What!!!*

*Girls night?*

*My cousin's wedding planning thing is tonight. But I will ditch early and come see you.*

I groan out loud.

"The case is that bad, Ms. Fox?" Flowers voice startles me and I drop my phone.

I turn my eyes to the open case file on my desk and heave a sigh of relief. At least it's open. I have no idea what it says, but I could have been staring at the closed cover for half an hour for all I know.

"The groan was more a—"

He cuts me off. "I don't really care. I came to let you know that you get to clean the child's corner of the family law courtrooms tonight. Since you made my list."

I blink. The gooey, sticky toys in the family law waiting area? Where hairballs coughed up by were-children roll around like tumbleweeds? Where swamp things leave their soggy children while they argue over whose bog is better? "Sounds like a dream."

"Don't worry. I'll come up with something even more exciting tomorrow." He gives an evil grin and leaves.

I stand up, suddenly wishing I'd taken Ben up on his offer. On all his offers. My eyes water.

"Hey," Becca's voice rings out. "If you want to talk—"

I shake my head. "I'm good, thanks." She's sweet. But she's no JR.

I sigh and go to get my supplies from maintenance. At least scrubbing is mindless.

I step into the elevator with a bucket, bleach, and many, many sets of gloves. Investigation is the top floor. I have to go down eight to get to family. But, three floors down, on the level of the felony courtrooms, the elevator stops and opens.

"Well, if this isn't deja vu…"

I glance up and do a double take. Luke Hawkins (aka Hot Vamp to my pervy mind) steps into the elevator. He's in a crisp blue three-piece suit. The suit makes his blue eyes pop. His hair brushes his shoulders, a dark golden blond. He smiles and bam! Dimples. Dream-worthy dimples. He's like my own personal fantasy come to life.

I wait too long to respond, just staring like the horny, dimwitted twelve-year-old girl I've suddenly become.

"I heard you got a promotion," Luke nods toward my bucket, a shit-eating grin on his face.

I take a glove and toss it at his face.

"Shut it."

He catches the glove and smiles. "Seriously, Sarah didn't tell me you were working maintenance. I'd have dropped by after hours." He licks his lips and flashes his fangs.

"Yes, watching me scrub toilets would be so hot."

"Watching you bend over to scrub toilets would be hot," he winks.

I can't help it. I laugh. And a little bit of the pain from the Bennett disaster recedes.

"Wait. You're talking to my neighbor?"

Hawkins and I had gone on a date a little over a month ago. But just one. One glorious date. But his recent break up with his ex, a murder accusation, and my subsequent hook up with Bennett had quashed the prospect of another.

"Mrs. Snow is a sweet old lady. Plus, she's my informant."

"For what?"

He raises his eyebrows and stares at me. "What do you think I want information on?"

I feel giddy. He's been keeping tabs on me? Normally, that would be creepy. But, somehow, this makes me swoon.

He takes a step closer. I can feel the energy crackling between us. A month ago, I would have run for the hills rather than let him touch me. But right now, I'm not thinking straight. I'm not sure my brain is thinking at all. It's rather blood deprived. Because all my blood seems to have rushed to my—

"Lyon," he whispers. "You've been on a break with Bennett for a month. When are you going to go out with me?"

His words send erotic shivers down my spine. And the truth pops out of my mouth before I can contain it.

"We were on a break. We just broke up for real this evening."

His expression changes immediately. Sympathy crosses his face. His hand comes up but he stops short of touching me. "Can I?"

I don't let vamps touch me as a rule. A very big important rule since my blood can turn them human. But this is just a hug. In a public elevator. No need to panic, I tell my stupid heart. I'm not sure if it's pumping hard in anticipation or fear. But I want that hug. I need a hug. So, I nod.

Luke engulfs me, wrapping his arms around me lightly. It feels so good. Like hot chocolate on a rainy day good. I avoided this why? It's amazing. I'm sad when he pulls away.

"So, what's with the bucket? You Head of Maintenance, now?"

I appreciate his smooth change of subject to lighten the mood.

"Punishment. My spell casting sucks." The elevator dings for my floor. "This is me. I get to scrub all the kiddie toys here." I step off the elevator reluctantly.

The doors start to shut. But then Luke's hand stops them.

"Hey," he bites his lip. "Do you want some company?"

I scrunch my eyebrows. "What?"

"Do you want someone to ramble and keep your mind off things?"

A half-smile lights my face. "I'm not ready to—"

"Not a date," he holds up his hands, but immediately has to stick one out again to keep the elevator doors from closing.

"You're sure?"

"Yeah. Ly, I don't just want to date you. I like you. As a person."

Oh, cupcakes and gummy bears and marshmallows and everything squishy. Does he know what that statement just did to my insides?

"You want to watch me clean toys?"

"Yeah."

"Okay." I'm a little nervous as he steps off the elevator to stand beside me.

"Where to?" His smile's as wide as the Mississippi.

I jerk my head left and he starts following me down the hall.

"Ly," he starts.

"Yeah?"

"Full disclosure. This is just a friend thing. But if you bend over, I'm still gonna check out your ass."

I laugh. "Deal."

He sits in a chair and listens to me gripe about the Academy and Flowers—his stupid assignment to lose things. I avoid talking about Bennett. Until it slips out that he offered to get me out of this punishment.

Luke's eyes widen. "What'd you say?"

"I told him no! I want to earn my place." I grouse as I pull bright orange slime balls off the wall.

Luke doesn't respond for a second. When I turn to look at him, he's gripping the chair handles so hard, I'm worried he might break them.

"Are you okay?"

"I want to kiss you so bad right now it hurts." Luke breathes. He shakes his head, "Who says that anymore? Most people just want to climb the ladder. Get their break. It doesn't matter how. But you …"

He stands and walks over to me. I turn into him, until we're just a breath apart. His eyes flicker all over my face. "Don't let him change that about you. It's rare. Integrity." His eyes search mine. "It's precious."

"Okay." My lips somehow mutter the words. I have no idea how. Because my mind is floating in space. Almost like I'm tipsy. On a compliment.

Luke holds my eyes for another second. "But … anyway. Back to being just friends."

I giggle.

He groans and backs away. "God, burp or something. Make yourself less attractive. You're killing me."

I hold up the collection of slime balls in my hand. "Does the fact that my arm's covered in monster spit help?"

"A little." He sinks back into his seat.

I tell him stories about JR, trying to help him get back to our friend-zone. Because as much as I would love to kiss him right now, my heart's still a pulverized mess inside. Not ready.

When I run out of breath, Luke takes over. He tells me about his work while I put on a new set of gloves and scrub toys. He used to work at the shipyard, once upon a time. That got him some contacts abroad. Which led him to start importing custom casters. Which I thought meant wizards, but it turns out they're just wheels. He exports them all around the US for boring shit like shopping carts.

"That's a job?"

"It's twenty jobs. I have a whole team of employees who assemble and ship 'em." Luke leans forward in his seat.

"No way! Who does that? Trolls? Golems? I cannot imagine twenty people who would want such a mind-numbing job."

Luke laughs. "I think you're overestimating the general population's intelligence."

"Oh. So, *humans* work for you." I rib him. Lots of races think humans are stupid. I'm not one of those. But …

"I used to be human."

"Case in point," I wink.

A squeaky dog toy hits me on the shoulder.

"Hey! That was clean!" I toss it back at him. And add a dirty stuffed witch for good measure.

Bad move.

Suddenly I'm getting pummeled with toys. I squeal, using one arm for cover. I use the other to frantically toss toys back his way.

I lose. By a big margin. Because Luke takes an entire tub of toys and dumps it over my head.

"Truce!" I cry.

"Shake on it," he holds out his hand.

I reach for it but can't resist. At the last minute I pull him down. He ends up sprawled on top of me. An occasion I have most definitely imagined. In very naughty detail. But this is not that. On the upside, I'm not panicking at his touch. On the downside, there is some kind of toy in between us making a squeaky flatulent sound.

"Not it!" I shout and put my fingers on my forehead in the universal 'I-didn't-fart' signal.

He starts laughing. "Alright, Ly. You win." He shoves off me, and to my surprise plops down next to me and grabs a rag.

"What are you doing? You're gonna ruin your suit!"

"Well, I just ruined all your hard work. So I owe it to you to help out. That's what friends do, right?"

His eyes meet mine. And then I'm light-headed. I feel like there's too much oxygen in the room. Or not enough. I don't know. All I know is this: it's very tempting to imagine being more than friends with Luke.

3

At seven a.m. I meet JR at Wendel's, my fave fifties diner. It's one of my go-to restaurants. The baker there, Cherry Jones, is a master. Instead of fries and shakes and skulls, she's expanded the menu to a delicious assortment of desserts for all creatures. Her prowess has made me try all sorts of things I'd normally never touch. Examples? Candy Salad. (Result: Best way to have "vegetables" ever is when they're made out of sugar.) Fried Coconut and Hay. (The coconut part was delish.) Zombie pie. (Not a winner. Even though it's sprinkled in powdered sugar.)

I join JR in line, eyeing a couple of chocolate eclairs in the display case that are screaming my name. The night was too crazy for me to go out on a limb food-wise. I need good old-fashioned sweets for dinner.

"Ugh. I've been promoted," JR pouts out her lower lip. Which of course causes one of the workers to drop his tray. She's a nymph. A buxom brunette nymph who can bring just about any species of guy to heel. (Not that she does—I'd puke and we'd never be friends because I'd be constantly writhing in a sea of jealousy and self-pity.) Wait, what did she say? Oh, promotion. Right.

"OMG! You're gonna be in Investigations too!" I squeal and smash her into a hug.

"No. Not at work. For my cousin's wedding." She paws at me until I let her go.

"What? How do you get promoted at a wedding?"

"I'm now the *lucky* maid of honor." JR almost spits flames as she says the word lucky.

"What? Why?"

"Because the meeting was horrible. My cousin's a shrew. Camila fired her maid of honor over napkin rings."

"You're joking."

"Not joking."

"A little bit joking?"

She shakes her head. "Napkin rings."

"Dang."

We order, get my desserts, and make our way to a corner booth, JR shooting complaints rapid-fire.

"Slow down. I didn't hear that last one."

"She's got everything all catawampus. Nothing easy. And the wedding's in five days!"

"Ouch."

"We're gonna be pulling our hair out!" JR shakes her head, then steals a bite of my eclair. "I don't know how we're gonna do it."

We? She just said we? Who is this we? "Um, are you forgetting I have the Academy *and* work?"

JR grabs my collar and pulls me so we are nose to nose. "So help me, you are not leaving me alone in this, Ly-ly." Her eyes have a steely glint.

"But—"

"I have one word for you. Tattoo. I'm sure everyone at your office would love to hear about it." She hisses through her teeth.

"I'd never leave you on your own."

"That's what I thought."

I sigh. "I'll just ask Mrs. Snow to whip me up a Wacky Wakey spell."

"Yoo-hoo? Did I hear my name, sugar?" Mrs. Snow, my sweet and nosy—isn't it odd how those two traits seem to go together—neighbor and local wannabe witch doctor, totters over. She's wearing a bright green fern print dress. And she has a feather in her hair. You can take the prima donna out of the South but not the South outta the prima donna. She's never been able to shed her southern belle style.

Of course, as usual, Tabby Blue—my hero and a naughty elderly cat shifter with an eye for shifter men—is hot on Sarah Snow's heels. She doesn't have fashion sense, she wears coke-bottle thick glasses and practical leather shoes instead of heels, but she's got enough attitude for fifty women. I swear those two have become connected at the hip. Probably from all the gossiping they do over my love life. I haven't been able to go home for the past five weeks without hearing about Bennett or Luke.

I stifle a groan. I so do not want to talk about guys right now.

"Mind if we join?" Mrs. Snow's question is rhetorical as she's already slid her butt into the booth.

"I'm Tabby," Tabby holds out a hand to JR. "I've seen you over at Lyon's but I don't think we've met."

JR gives her a warm smile. And when JR smiles, ice melts. "I've heard so much about you. Lyon admires you so much."

Tabby puffs up with pride. She slides in next to JR.

Great. We're effectively trapped between two busybodies. And my heart just saw more explosive action than a splinter cat blasting trees in a forest. Time to make an offensive maneuver.

"JR has less than a week to put together a wedding for a bridezilla. Any ideas?"

A wedding will turn nearly any woman's head. But toss that term out to Sarah Snow and it's like she's won the lottery.

"Oh! I know just the thing. I've got a calming serum in my purse," she plonks a massive purse down in front of us. "We can use that to tone that bride down. Does she have her china patterns picked? Flowers? What all needs doing?"

JR and Sarah start speaking 'girl.' I tune out.

I'll help. I will. Especially after that threat. But is it wrong to want a minute to wallow? In the breakup with Bennett and/or the subsequent amazingness of Luke?

Tabby's throat clearing signals that I will not, in fact, get to wallow. At all. "So, Ly—"

I hurry to interrupt what could be a romance-related question. "Weren't you telling me one time about how you enchanted a balloon to look like you or something to get out of class?"

Tabby narrows her eyes, sensing a diversion. But I toss on a compliment, hoping that will help keep her on the track I want.

"It's just that was such a brilliant plan, you know? Like I wish I'd thought of it. Wish I could use it during our exercises each night but then I'd fail the Academy, because they intersperse their tests. You think JR could get away with it?" I'm rambling, crossing my fingers that Tabby bites.

She does.

"Yes, I used that decoy to get out of astral projection class. Such a waste of time. Sit there like you're sleeping and send your soul somewhere else. Anyone could come up and do anything to you! Stupidest thing. Why do that when there are crystal balls?" She pauses to grin at the waiter dropping off JR's food.

"I'll have a bowl of milk, please and thank you young man," she puts in her order, never-minding the fact that you're supposed to pre-pay at the counter. I don't think Tabby cares too much about rules. Not if her arrest record is anything to go by.

"Anyway, I used to sneak off to watch the were-lions hunt," her expression gets dreamy.

Good. She's totally off on a tangent that's not my life. Dodged a bullet. Whew.

"Anyway, dear," Tabby shakes herself out of memory and pats me on the hand, "That enchantment's called a balloon decoy. And the spell to animate it is pretty complex. It might take me two or three days to cast."

I jerk my head toward JR. "I'm pretty sure she's gonna be clawing her eyes out in two or three days."

Tabby scratches her chin. "Well, I guess I could always check Gor's Pawnshop."

"You go there?" My eyes widen. Gor's is a rough place. Run by a goblin. Known to fence stolen goods. I prepped a couple of cases against him back when I was a paralegal.

"They have all kinda things there second-hand. Much cheaper than the big-box. They got muzzles, leashes, and handcuffs—"

"Stop! Stop!" I hold up a hand, then quickly cover my ears in case Tabby doesn't comply. I'm am so scared right now that I'm about to get a run-down on were-cat BDSM.

Thankfully, the waiter comes back with Tabby's bowl of milk. I toss him a gold coin to pay for the bowl and as a thank you for saving my mind from experiencing permanent trauma.

Sarah and JR take over the conversation at that point, creating a very complex calendar of events that somehow, I'm just supposed to remember.

I try not to let my eyes glaze over.

Sarah starts describing some potion she'll whip up to help JR with last minute details. I think my ears go numb from all the talking.

So when Cherry Jones, my cooking idol, pops out of the kitchen, I see my chance to escape.

"Cherry!" I call. Mrs. Snow scoots out of the booth so I can get out. I cross the busy diner to shake her hand.

She squints her eyes at me trying to remember who I am.

I put the poor unicorn shifter out of her misery. "I'm Lyon. Luke Hawkins' friend. We met a couple weeks ago."

Recognition dons in her purple eyes. "You're the one he's pining over."

I chuckle uncomfortably. "I guess. I'm using the fact that I met you once to escape wedding planning over there."

Cherry's eyes bounce over my friends. "Smart move. I had to come out to meet a catering client. Big parties are chaos." She shakes her rainbow hair from side to side and it's like a salon commercial for the supernatural. For a second, I wish I was a unicorn. Who wouldn't?

"Big parties, big drama," I toss back. "What kind are you catering?"

Cherry rolls her eyes. "Some ridiculous combination retirement-slash-promotion party. I guess this guy is up for a promo, but if he doesn't get it, he'll retire. Or something. I dunno. His wife's crazy. Wants to go sail around the world or some whacko thing like that." She shudders. "I can't even imagine getting in the ocean. Night*mare!*" She makes a little shuddering noise reminiscent of a whinny.

"Yeah, that wouldn't be my retirement dream," I agree, though I don't have her equine aversion to the ocean. I'd just much rather read.

"Oh, there she is," Cherry nods toward an overweight woman with a purse the size of a concrete block and beak of a nose. Bright blue leaches through the skin on her nose, drawing even more attention to the unattractive feature. (I'm guessing she's shifter. Leaching can happen with older shifters. Can't hold their shape. Just like some old people can't hold their bladder.) The woman has to turn sideways to get in the door.

"I'll let you get to it then," I sigh. I glance back at my table, where discussions are still full force. Damn.

A hand grabs my arm. Cherry's eyes have grown as big as a baby doll's. They overpower her face. "Lyon, this might be overstepping. But do not miss your shot. I hear Luke's average O ratio is three to one."

Did she just say what I think she said? No. She's got to be talking about blood type or something, right? "I'm sorry. I think I misheard—"

"You didn't. He's legendary. Mythical even." She winks and walks away.

OMG. I already knew I wasn't going to be able to sleep. But now, I won't even be able to close my eyes.

Luke Hawkins just got labeled a sex unicorn.

## 4

Three nights later. I haven't made it off Flower's list. Haven't lost any yoga blocks in his office. (He caught me trying to plant one. Did not go over well.) I haven't slept because I'm helping JR with tulle and centerpiece crap 'til noon every frickin' day. Mrs. Snow's potions don't help me at all (and they taste like vinegar, so I kinda stopped taking them). But I'm too cheap to go buy Peppy Perk Potion because it's like sixty gold. Gah!

And now, Flowers has come up with the worst punishment assignment to date. At least tonight, I share the bottom listing with Seena and Becca.

We're on crowd control. A shit-job if there ever was one. Standing around with a badge on my chest so that it makes this event look more important. Like eight people are here on the floor. Eight! Crowd control for eight people? Seriously. I'd rather be cleaning bathrooms. How does he stand still for so long? I glare at Flowers, who looks totally at ease in his "guard" stance.

I curl my toes in my shoes.

We have been here at Town Hall for two hours, standing around doing nothing. Literally nothing. I've counted the columns. I've stared up at the balcony on the second floor. I now have memorized the portraits of our founding fathers. Did you know a kraken supposedly helped found Tres Lunas? Yeah. Hmm. I'm a little skeptical. We're only half an hour from the ocean, but still. How'd he get here? Methinks some scholar got it wrong. Or some painter played a practical joke.

I turn my eyes back to the stage and sigh at the ridiculousness of my current situation. I weigh it versus the kraken.

There are more people lining the stage up there than sitting in the crowd: current City Council members, mayor's assistants, and miscellaneous bigwigs all want their moment to shine on camera. In fact, I'm pretty sure all the people sitting in our "crowd" are executive assistants to the jerks on stage. Possibly the hair and makeup crew for the stupid nymph news reporter, Jackie Hanna, who's been interviewing everyone for the past hour. I deliberately avoid eye contact with her as she sashays around the stage. But I can't help noticing she's wearing a ring. A huge emerald. God, don't tell me someone's stupid enough to put a ring on *that*.

"Why, Councilman Max," Jackie purrs, bending forward to give the camera a good cleavage shot, "Do you have any predictions as to who Mayor Honeycutt will select as the new Council Member?"

Max is the only familiar ever to be elected to City Council. He's a Siamese cat who's worked with fourteen wizards over the course of his career. But of course, all his magical achievements are forgotten. All anyone remembers about him now is that he was on a commercial for a cat-food company.

Max licks his back leg and declines to comment. I figure that's the feline version of 'Eff you.' I mean, he couldn't get much closer to licking his butt on camera without paying obscenity fines. I decide I like him.

Jackie's not sure how to react. She bites her lip and gets a little lipstick on her teeth. Her cameraman instantly stops the shot and goes up to tell her. An assistant runs up with a mirror and fixes her up.

In the meantime, her cameraman goes to his bag of equipment, rustles through some cords, curses, then heads past me.

I watch him pull open the door to the hall behind me. But even as he pulls open the door, someone pushes it open. Someone in a bright orange sweat suit.

"Lyon! Lyon, we made it!" Mrs. Snow and Tabby scurry around the cameraman and give me hugs.

Sarah's been helping with wedding sweatshop—our pet name for Camila's never-ending list of tasks for JR. She knew I'd be here tonight working. (Probably because I spent half the morning whining about it.)

Unlike me, Sarah squealed when I told her about guard duty for the appointment of the new City Councilor—like I'd invited her to the prom. (Note to self, get hobbies when I retire. Or shit like this will be exciting times.)

And now Sarah's here. With Tabby. Well, at least the night's looking less boring for me.

"Guess what!" Sarah yells through the hall, oblivious to everyone who turns to stare. "I finished that Pause Potion for JR!" She holds up a little vial like it's an award.

Tabby pants and holds her chest as they near me. "Whew, thought we'd miss it. Anything big happen?"

I shake my head no.

Sarah Snow smiles. "Lucky for us, a sweet young vamp just happened to give us a lift."

I inhale sharply and look behind them. There, striding confidently up the hall, is the vamp version of perfection. Luke wears tight black jeans and a black t-shirt. No jacket, despite the fall chill. Benefit of being undead. But the other benefit, the one I care more about, is the view of his biceps, covered in hot rune tattoos. His long blond hair is loose, framing his face. When our eyes meet, his dimples pop out with his smile. Cherry's last words to me echo in my head. And my panties are suddenly burned to a crisp. Damn. Can you say ultimate temptation?

"Lyon, you are on duty." Flowers evil voice in my ear-piece cuts off my fantasies of long hot bouts of nakedness with Luke's hair brushing my neck.

A flush creeps over my cheeks. I smile at Sarah and Tabby. I give Luke a tentative grin. "Glad you could make it. As you can see, there are plenty of seats. But I have to get back to work."

"Work?" Tabby raises an eyebrow. "There's not enough people here to spit on. Where's that boss of yours?" She tromps over to the other side of the room, a woman on a mission. My eyes follow her, glowing in admiration.

Luke takes a step forward. I hold up a hand to stop him.

"Take a good look at her. Re-think this whole dating thing. Because she is exactly who I want to be in fifty years."

Luke chuckles.

51

We hear Tabby ripping into Flowers. I meet Luke's eyes. "I'm totally serious."

"I know." His eyes flit over my face. Admiration, amusement, lust cross his features. Somehow, I know what each one of his micro-expressions is. Which is crazy. Because we hardly know each other. We've been on one date. One date, where I was secretly digging for info about his ex-girlfriend, the vamp I was accused of murdering. One date where I got him to admit his food fetish and ended up in his lap … okay, okay, I'm making it dirtier in my mind than it actually was. But it still was so, so—my feet are drawn toward him like magnets are pulling us together. Our recent friendly play in the kiddie area of the courthouse floods my mind.

I'm pretty sure he can read my thoughts because he flashes me a naughty grin.

Sarah's clap and giggle jerk me out of my heated state. She's watching us like a giddy little cupid. I clear my throat.

"I really got to get back to work. Enjoy the show, guys."

"Wait. I wanted to ask you something." Luke steps toward me and uses his back to shield me from the crowd.

"What is it?"

"Maybe I shouldn't—" a blush stains his neck.

I've never seen him nervous. It's adorable. I put a hand on his arm. And feel absolutely no vampire-induced fear whatsoever. Damn. I'm far gone. I try to ease his mind. "Hey, whatever it is, it can't be worse than the expanding underwear Tabby tried to pawn off on me."

That earns a chuckle. "She didn't."

"No. She would though."

Luke clears his throat. But a nervous scratch remains. "I thought I might help you practice losing things sometime."

"What kind of things?" My answer is way too suggestive for the friend facade we're trying to maintain.

He takes a step closer. I think my response dissolved his nerves. "I have some ideas."

"Not gonna tell me?"

He shakes his head slowly. "Anticipation is half the fun." He winks.

"When?"

"In two nights? I should be free around four a.m."

"Sure."

A cat-call echoes through my earpiece. Seena's voice cackles through the wire.

"Loser got a date!"

Becca comes to my defense, though she's stationed across the room. "Shut it, Seena."

Things calm down for about two minutes. Luke takes a seat and eventually Flowers is able to get rid of Tabby.

He tells the three of us to converge near the front doors. Why? Who knows? But at least we can talk without him overhearing everything.

We watch Jackie's cameraman, who's back in action, attempt to avoid tripping over wires as he scurries to follow Jackie to all her interviews.

Seena leans over, "Five gold say he's gonna biff it."

Becca shakes her head. "No way, he's a pro."

Seena groans as the cameraman successfully navigates the cords leading to the podium and follows Jackie to interview our most senior Councilperson.

Councilwoman Jiang is the complete opposite of Max the Cat. She flits her perfect wings so she can hover next to Jackie. Jealous? Me? Never. I do not hate, at all, the way she has frosted her wing tips so they look like icicles and glitter under the camera lights. I embrace my wingless state. It's so much easier to ... get through doors. Yeah.

I force a smile as I listen to her make all kinds of ridiculous nothing statements about how she's sure Mayor Honeycutt has picked the most worthy candidate, the one who wants to help promote the good of our city ... blah blah blah.

I'm relieved when Giancarlo Russo, our vamp Councilor steps in. And no, it's not because his name rolls off the tongue in the seductive way cigarette ads used to make smoke roll off people's lips. It has nothing to do with his Italian accent. I'm just tired of the empty platitudes, thank you. It's hard enough to stand still with my legs apart and hands clasped and avoid looking at Luke every third second. I'd prefer to stay awake while I struggle to do those things.

I give a little sigh. Why is it that all vamps are smoldering hot? Russo might have turned vamp in his mid-forties, but hello. The silver hair at his temples only makes me wanna get kinky. Geez, focus, Ly. What's the matter with you? Job. Job. I really need to pay for that Peppy Perk Potion.

I am gonna have a hard time keeping my promise to JR not to date any vamps ever again. She made me swear not to touch vamps after I had some problems with a vamp ex of mine. Not to mention the blood thing. Sigh. I know she's right. But … my eyes drift to Luke.

He's steadily watching me.

I've been scared of dating vamps for a long, long time. I try to resurrect that fear while I look at him. But it just won't come.

I feel a tap on my shoulder. I turn to see the final Councilor, the white witch Clo, looking at me. And when I say white, I mean literally. Not race. Like paper white skin. White hair to her waist. Even her eyes are a scary bluish white that make her pupils look like black speck of dirt. If she didn't wear a ton of makeup, I'm pretty sure she'd look totally creepy. Lucky for me, she's rocking the blush for the camera.

"Excuse me. Do you think we could get some more water bottles? I think that we will probably need them." Clo gives a small smile and waves a hand toward the short list of appointees. "I think whichever of them gives a speech, might need a little to drink." She winks.

Ah. She's saying water. But she means vodka. I size her up.

She's pegged me as a rule-breaker. Not that it's *not* true, strictly speaking. But I'm not sure I like that. Or her.

She's supposedly a sweetheart, which means her intentions are as pure as snow. Sweethearts are the 'good' supernatural creatures. Good witches. Fae. Creatures like that. Is it weird I'm skeptical of that? That I don't trust that label? (Maybe it's because I break the mold for a fairy. Or JR breaks the nymphomaniac stereotype. Maybe I just like outcasts.)

I eye Clo for a second before turning to Becca.

"Sure, we can help. Becca, where's that kitchen area again?"

Becca bounds off, calling behind her, "I'll grab the waters!"

I'm not sure if she senses the tension between Clo and I or if she just wants and excuse to move. Either way works for me.

Clo eyes me for a moment before drifting back to the stage.

I turn my attention to the potential appointees. Jackie is now interviewing them.

Unlike the current City Councilors, the potential appointees onstage all look a little sick to their stomachs. There's a bald man with a walrus-sized mustache who's got beads of sweat all over his face.

A large woman scurries up to the stage with a handkerchief and starts dabbing. She looks familiar. When she turns, I know why.

She's got a hooked nose, big and blue. She's the one I saw meeting Cherry.

My eyes flicker back to her husband. What was that party for? Promo or retirement? Looking at him, retirement is more likely. He shuffles his feet awkwardly, jerks his shoulders a couple times, and straightens his tie more than once.

His words are a high-pitched breathy hiss when Jackie Hanna starts interviewing him on camera.

"Yes. Yes. Regulation of the airways is always going to be a … a top priority," he squeaks. "With witches, ghosts, shifter aviators all sharing the skies, we… we really gotta buckle down." He tries a forceful fist in hand motion at that point. It doesn't work at all. I almost feel sorry for him.

And then he ruins it.

"I mean, it clearly makes most sense for the corporeal to take precedence. Ghosts can fly through buildings for cripe's sake."

I exchange a look with Seena and roll my eyes. This dude's anti-ghost. Which ends up being anti-earthbound. Idiot. Read the news. Mondstark, Virginia tried that twenty years back. Chaos. Ghosts popping through walls. Freezing sleeping were-pups and scaring people in the shower. No. Clearly, ghosts belong in the sky.

I hope the mayor doesn't appoint this clown. His blue-nosed wife is right. It's time for him to retire.

I turn toward the other two potential appointees and tune out the man I'm now nicknaming Raspberry. Because he makes me want to blow one at him.

There's a pixie fluttering near Clo. She's got a shock of pink hair and at least six diamonds piercing her eyebrows. She smiles at Jackie, waiting for her turn to speak. Bleh. I don't really want her either. Pixies aren't my fave as a rule. Who else we got?

To my utter shock, I see Gor, the pawnshop goblin. Tabby's walked over and is talking right to him, like they're buddies. His grey elephant skin shakes as he speaks. His hooked nose might rival Raspberry's wife's. And his claws are the stuff of nightmares. Instinctively, I want to go drag Tabby away from him. But she'd probably hiss at me.

She shoves her glasses up her nose and laughs at something he says.

Could it be that the scary goblin is funny?

I've always thought the billboards with his face plastered all over them were a mistake. "A Pawn Shop You Can Trust." That's his motto. I always assumed he got hosed by some marketing company who put his face right next to those words. But was he being tongue-in-cheek? Should I like this guy?

Becca comes back in with an armful of water bottles and I stop pondering. I help her bring them to the stage. Clo wanders over with a couple minibar sized vodka bottles, waves her hand, and spells the vodka from one bottle into the other.

Raspberry grabs one and downs it. No 'thank you,' or nod of thanks or anything. Yeah. I named him well. That's why I don't bother to tell him that the water might make him tipsy.

"Everyone," Jackie claps her hands. "It's nearly time. Quick bathroom break to freshen up for the camera. Be back in five!" She claps her hands, like this is some pep rally. I wonder if she's got pompoms in that makeup bag of hers. Possible.

Her little assistant hefts a huge tote over her shoulder as everyone trots off toward the bathroom. Giancarlo tosses an arm around Jackie and escorts her from the room. I wonder if they have a private "interview" scheduled. Gah. I hate cheaters.

"Back to stations." Flowers hisses in my ear.

I roll my eyes but comply.

And five minutes later, once everyone's back, I know why he wanted us by the doors.

They burst open.

The mayor's security bats fly in. They take up position on the chandeliers. And then the mayor enters.

David Honeycutt strides in with the force and confidence of a tornado. At the DA's office, people used to label his moods. "Watch out. He's an F-5 today." Even now, when he's not angry, Honeycutt clears a path in front of him. Guess one of the advantages of being a minotaur is intimidation. Even Flowers looks cowed.

Jackie Hanna and her cameraman scurry off the stage and take up position a few rows down.

"Coming to you live from Town Hall, I'm Jackie Hanna. Mayor Honeycutt is about to announce the new City Councilor. The fifth seat has been open for seven months, since the passing of Lou Strip, beloved zebra-shifter. Joining the Council is a lifetime position. We covered the story when the last two potential appointees were murdered and disqualified for corruption. You can find those stories online. In light of those issues, the mayor is exercising his right to appoint the new Council member. Whomever the mayor selects will have a major influence on the laws of Tres Lunas for decades to come. The mayor's ascending the stage now."

The mayor paws the ground and snorts before he takes the stage and stands at the podium. (I'm slightly fascinated because they always cut that part out on TV broadcasts. I wonder why? Does he want to appear more human on TV?)

After the required 'I'm about to make a speech so shut the hell up' throat clearing, Honeycutt smiles. "Today, I'm proud to announce that our City Council will be joined by an esteemed member of Tres Lunas. Our City Council has always been a balance of opinions in order to represent the needs of our diverse citizens. That's why I'm so proud to announce today's appointee."

Onstage, the pixie works to keep a smile on her face. If the mayor's talking about balance, he's picked a dark heart. With only five seats and a white witch and fairy on board, the Council has two sweethearts. Technically, Max the Cat is considered a neutral party. So, another dark heart makes sense. Bummer for her.

Mayor Honeycutt continues his address, "He's spent over twenty years building his own business, been a solid family man."

Does Gor have a family? I eye the goblin. He sees me and gives a little sharp-toothed grin. One that makes me wish I had covers. And a nightlight.

Quickly, I turn to Raspberry. He's sweating again. This time the sweat is rolling off him in buckets. Sheets. Like his own personal rainstorm. Ew.

Honeycutt does that annoying dramatic pause thing. Where the only people interested are the candidates. "Please give a big round of applause for—"

Before he can announce the winner, Raspberry falls forward, flat on his face.

## 5

**R**aspberry's wife shrieks and rushes toward him. "Bernard!"

Most of the rest of us stand around uncertainly, me included.

Not Becca. She rushes up the aisle, jumps onstage, and shoves her fingers onto the guy's neck.

His wife tries to push her away, but Becca snaps. "Do you want me to check his pulse or not?"

I share a grin with Seena. Looks like little Becca has some claws.

Then I push on my ear piece to activate the mic. "Boss. Anything you want us to do?"

Flowers takes a minute to respond. "I called the paramedics. So just stand by."

Becca declares Bernard will live. Apparently, he's just fainted.

I put another tic in the "winner" column for him.

Seena and I wander toward the stage, since Flowers is on his phone. We want a glimpse of the fainter close up.

"Bet it was Jackie's boobs. Probably the most action he's seen in years," Seena whispers as we approach the stage.

I snicker.

Almost everyone onstage sat back down after Becca's declaration.

But not Jackie, who's leaning into the camera and doing a low volume play-by-play for the five retired people watching this at home.

And not the wife. Bernard's wife is absolutely ridiculous. She's waggling her arms and raising Cain. "Where are the paramedics? Is there a shifter-doctor here? Oh, I knew this pressure would be too much for him."

Mrs. Snow and Tabby come up beside me.

"Well, sugar, this has turned into quite the exciting event!" Mrs. Snow giggles.

Tabby shrugs. "Woulda' been cooler if he died."

Sarah slaps her shoulder. "Don't say that!"

"Where's Luke?" I turn to look for him.

"Oh, he had to leave honey. Said he had to get to work."

I nod. Guess wheels don't roll themselves.

A couple of medics come through a side door. That was quick. Hmm. There are perks to fainting on camera in town hall.

They rush over to Bernard, who's starting to sit up, bleary-eyed.

Jackie and her cameraman crowd the paramedics, so they can get everyone into the shot. I roll my eyes. Part of me wants to push Jackie and her Channel 13 goon away. But nobody else says boo. So I guess this is the downside of fainting in front of the mayor.

"How many fingers am I holding up?" A paramedic asks Raspberry.

"Three."

"What's your name?"

"Bernard Bell."

"What species are you?"

"I'm a were-booby."

A snort escapes. I can't help it. I quickly turn around. Beside me, Seena does the same.

"He said booby on TV," I crow as we speed walk away from the stage.

"Were-booby? What the hell is a were-booby?" Seena asks. "Does he transform into a giant breast?"

Becca joins us. "If he does, I hope he opened a topless joint. That would be awesome."

Flowers comes over to our snickering cluster. He does not look happy. "What are you doing?"

Between chuckles I remind him. "Were-booby? Did you not just hear that?" My ribs will hurt from holding in the laughter. So much laughter. So inappropriate. I wish more people were here. I wish for a crowd to hide in. So I could just bust out.

"You imbeciles," Flowers' tone is scathing. "A booby is a type of sea-bird."

He thinks it helps. But I just snort again. "You said booby, too." I am at that point of exhaustion where things that should just be meh-funny are frickin' hilarious.

"Look, they've got their hands all over the booby. On camera." Seena points at the medics. At this point, he's giving off tiny hiccups with his laughs.

"Get into the hall and calm down," Flowers lectures. "You have sixty seconds to get yourselves together. This is completely unprofessional."

I pinch my lips together and hurry toward the double doors.

I smack into Giancarlo's assistant as I do so.

He's too busy yapping into the phone to look at me. "Yes. He'll be late to the hunt. Some bozo here had a medical emergency. No. Fainted. Yeah, I know. Everything's packed—"

"Sorry," I rub my shoulder.

The guy just rolls his eyes at me and keeps walking. Geez. Dude. It's called an accident.

The hit sobers me up a little, but Seena's still having problems. He sinks onto the floor in the hall, holding his sides.

"Okay, okay, it's funny. Come on, we gotta get back in there," Becca urges.

Seena can't focus.

Becca stomps her little foot. "Seena! Come on! You don't want to be on Flower's list tomorrow, do you?"

He's out of control. I don't really know what to do to stop him. Because watching him just makes me want to laugh all over again.

"Hey!" Becca snaps in his face. "Would you want everyone laughing at your were-animal?"

That shuts him up. Seena turns a threatening glare on Becca.

I look back and forth between the two, fascinated. I think back to our magic sessions at the gym. I've never seen Seena shift. He's pretty good with spell work. Says it's like coding. So he's always worked on that. I never really thought about it before. But why hasn't he shifted? What does he turn into? And why does Becca know?

"I'm a stallion!" he hisses at her, so softly I have to strain to hear it.

"I'm pretty sure there's a size requirement for that label," Becca whispers back.

"Wait…" I put two and two together. I turn to Seena. "Are you a … pony?" I clap.

His nostrils flare. "I'm an Arabian *horse*."

"Miniature," Becca winks and pokes his rib. She turns to me. "He's white and like three feet tall."

My jaw drops. "OMG. This assignment is turning into the best thing ever! First, there's a booby. And now I find out Seena's a little pony."

"I've been calling him MLP," Becca winks at me.

"Stop," Seena warns.

I hold up a hand. "We'll stop. We have to go back to work. Or Flowers is gonna kick our behinds." I turn to Becca. "You know we have to get him drunk and draw an ice cream cone on his butt at Halloween now, right?"

Becca's eyes light up. "Totally."

Grumpy Seena throws open the doors and stomps back in, ready to work.

I, on the other hand, have to focus very hard on containing my bliss. This assignment might be the highlight of my new job.

Of course, as soon as I think that, everything has to go to shit.

The mayor's pulled Bernard aside and is trying to convince him to go home. Bernard the Booby is having none of it.

"I'm fine!" he roars, clearly forgetting that his loss of temper is on camera. Jackie and her guy are lapping it up.

"Look, there's really no reason for you to stay when you're clearly having a health issue."

"I—what? You picked him?" He waves an incredulous arm at Gor the Goblin, who looks as smug as anyone with that awful a mug can look. "How much did he pay you, huh? Or was it the Crypts? They funding him, too? Just like your little vacation to Maui—" His bald, chubby face is turning red with rage. Like a raspberry. (Damn I'm good with names.)

I see Tabby stand up nearby. She marches over to Bernard and grabs his ear. "You big whiner. I don't wanna hear another chirp outta you! He's doing an exec's job managing a city of hundreds of thousands of people. Of course, he's gonna take bribes, you idiot! His salary's jack! But does he do a good job? Does he? How low's the troll murder rate gotten, huh?" She yanks him by the ear.

Bernard rears back to hit Tabby and she shifts. In public. On camera! One second, she looks like a sweet old lady. Then the magic is swirling around her, clothes are shredded on the floor, and an orange cat with a notch in one ear is perched on Bernard's shoulders.

He reacts as any seabird would. With utter panic.

He screams, flapping his arms, and running straight into the rows of unused plastic chairs in the audience. His wife screams and chases after them, using her purse to swat at Tabby. The mayor's security bats hear the frantic noise and start swooping down around the group.

I hear Seena's voice in my ear. "Uh, boss? Should we …"

I do not want to have to arrest Tabby.

"It's technically assault, but she's in a form that's a tenth of his size, " Flowers replies. "D.A. won't file it. And she shifted in self-defense, so … what I really hope is the news has a five-second delay so they can cut that part out."

Becca's voice is next. "What about his wife?"

Flowers exhales loudly. I see him take a step toward the chaos. "Hey!" he yells. But that's as far as he gets.

The wife's purse is about to brain Tabby when she jumps off Bernard. The purse whacks him instead.

Man, Tabby's got good reflexes. She lands on her feet and trots off like that brawl was nothing, remaining in her cat form. (Thank goodness.) She perches next to Sarah Snow and starts to bathe, all collected cat confidence. I glance around the room. Almost everyone is exchanging incredulous looks. Max the Cat's eyes are glued on Tabby. Uh-oh. Ew. I do not want to think about his reaction to that little display.

And by little display, I mean fight.

Bernard Bell definitely got the worse end of the deal. His suit's torn up and he's got a welt on his forehead—not sure if it's from his wife's purse or the fall he took earlier. Either way, he looks awful. He pushes away his fussing wife with her handkerchiefs and straightens his suit. He stomps back onto the stage and stands next to the other potential appointees. His chest is heaving.

"What is he doing?" Becca whispers to me.

"I'm pretty sure he doesn't realize this is being aired live."

She rolls her eyes.

"He thinks he can stand there and they'll just re-tape the announcement?" Seena's incredulous.

"Guess so."

I check my phone. Scenes of the fight are already popping up on Instaghoul.

Jackie and her cameraman return to their places in the aisle.

"The desire for that City Council spot has tempers flaring! One of the potential appointees has even accused our own mayor of corruption! Politics at its worst, or best. You decide. We still await the official announcement of the next City Councilor, a position that lends great legislative power to the holder."

The mayor glares daggers at Bernard for the accusations, and then at Jackie for repeating them. But he maintains his cool. He sends his security bats flying off to a side room to cool down. They're just trying to land on everyone's hair in here.

Then Honeycutt returns to the podium. He skips all pretense this time and states, "I'm proud to announce that Gor the Goblin will be joining the City Council—" he puts an arm out to welcome Gor to come shake his hand.

Jackie swings her arm toward Gor like a model showcasing a new crystal ball on some game show.

Gor takes a step forward.

Bernard grabs Gor by the shoulder, spinning the man and fiercely shaking his hand. I think he might be trying to crush it.

"Congra—," he's having trouble pretending to be a good sport. I roll my eyes. In the millisecond that takes, half the room goes nuts.

Suddenly, the mayor's hands are over his ears and he's hunched over. Max the Cat is hissing, Tabby's back is arched, hair standing on end. The bats are back, swooping. Seena's snorting and running toward a side door. Flowers is crouched ready to pounce, scanning the crowd. In other words—WTF? Half the people in the room have just gone crazy. There's chaos.

Becca and I exchange confused looks. I shoot her a "What the hell?" eyebrow raise. She responds with a shrug and jogs over to check on Seena, who's pawing at a door handle like he forgot how to open it. His animal fear has totally won out. Looks like he's running on horse instinct.

The mayor's snorting.

Flowers is the first to come out of his crouch and resume standing.

I touch my mic. "What's going on?" I hope Flowers has some answers. Because I'm lost as to what caused this moment of panic. What would make all the shifters and animals go nutso?

Before Flowers can answer me, a gargled sound catches everyone's attention. All eyes turn toward Bernard.

The Booby is still standing on stage. His eyes are wide. And it looks like he's struggling to breathe. He falls face-first onto the stage. Again.

A chorus of groans arise.

Flowers left his mic on and we can hear his sigh. "Dammit. I don't know what that was. You didn't hear it?"

"Nope," I reply.

"Maybe a mic went bad. Horrible noise." He pulls out his phone. "I'm calling the medics for Bell. They probably just got out of downtown."

Bell's wife, of course, goes into hysterics again. With the amount of fainting her husband does, you think she'd be used to it.

She flaps her hands and bends over him. "Bernard!"

Gor suddenly jumps back from where he stands next to them.

"He pissed himself."

Becca sprints up the aisle, or what's left of it, considering all the chairs Bernard knocked over.

She pulls out her phone, turns on the flashlight. She flips Bernard over and shines the light in his eyes.

"Non-responsive!" she calls out.

She reaches for his neck and sets her fingers on his pulse.

"I think he's dea—" her eyes go wide, and she looks up, staring at Seena in a panic.

Then sweet little Becca slumps over, eyes open, right on top of Bernard.

6

I'm in shock. I don't think I've blinked for like thirty seconds. What is going on?

But while my mind has shut my body down, other people have jumped up.

Sarah Snow, for instance. She jogged up to the stage and pulled Becca off Bernard the Booby. She grabbed a vial out of her purse. I vaguely recognize the pause potion before she dumps it all over Becca.

"Wait!" Flowers leaps onto the stage and snatches the vial out of Mrs. Snow's hand. "What are you doing?"

"It's a pause potion," she explains. "It'll stop whatever's going on."

Flowers closes his eyes and exhales through his nose. I think he's pissed at Sarah. "Go sit. Do not leave. Do not speak."

"It's obviously some enchantment."

"Do *not* speak!" The tiger in him becomes obvious as he steps into Sarah's space until she complies with a huff.

He turns to the mayor, "I'm sorry, but we're going to have to—"

Honeycutt nods, agreeing with whatever Flowers is about to say.

Jackie cuts in, shoving her microphone into Flower's face. "Sir. What's going on? Aren't you with Tres Lunas Police?"

"Yes," he replies gruffly. "And you need to turn that thing off. This is now the scene of a murder investigation."

Jackie gives a B-reel actress gasp.

Flowers waves at the cameraman, who complies and sets down the camera. But, I notice, the red blinking light on the back doesn't go off.

I trot over, grab the camera, and help him out.

"This," I gesture to the power button, "is how you actually turn off the video."

The geeky guy wears a name badge with Mason McDonelly, Channel Thirteen, on it. He blushes and shrugs. "My finger must notta pushed hard enough."

My eyes narrow as I turn off the video feed. "Yeah. Right."

Seena comes over, looking pale and shaken. His eyes leave Becca's for only a second to meet mine. "They could have a separate sound feed. We need to turn off all the audio equipment too."

"Good catch."

I get the happy job of stripping Jackie of her lav mic and searching to find the hidden video cameras in her earrings. Sorry girl. I've pulled that one before. I tug them off and check the rest of her. She's jewelry and spy-cam free now, so I head over to Flowers, who's made the entire City Council and the one odd pixie candidate sit onstage. He's casting echo spells on them. Pixie's the last in line. She tests hers out.

"Hello…lo..lo," her own voice echoes back to her. Common protocol, I learned it three weeks in. It's an easy way for us to prevent witnesses from talking to each other. Changing stories. I notice one person is missing from the stage.

"Where's the wife?"

Flowers eyes flit over the people onstage and he realizes Raspberry's wife isn't there. "Find her. Nobody else move!"

Even I would not disobey the threat in that voice. I've been on the receiving end of Flower's glare. Right now, I'm glad I'm on the other side. I trot next to him as we make our way around the room.

"Did you call for backup?"

"Yup."

"Medics?"

"Yup."

"Takeout?"

He turns to me and snarls. "This is not a joke! Someone's dead. Maybe two people."

"I know that. But we have over a dozen people to interview. Half of whom are smart enough not to answer anything without an attorney. So that is gonna take hours right there. And we need to get someone up here to take care of Jackie and the paper or we're gonna have chaos on our hands with the press. We're gonna be here until tomorrow. We need takeout."

I see his lip twist a little. He doesn't want to admit that I'm right. I fall back a step or two so he doesn't have to. But after a minute, Flowers grabs his phone and punches a speed-dial number. "Get takeout, too. Twenty people." He hangs up without another word.

Should I feel slightly victorious? No. Probably stupid to feel this way, but I do.

I walk closer. "How do you know it's a murder?" I ask. Because honestly, I'm still so lost as to what just happened.

Raspberry just fell down. "How do you know Bernard—" I resist saying booby, "didn't just have a heart attack?"

Flowers checks behind some ornamental curtains. "Becca wouldn't have passed out too. There has to be a spell involved. And there's no way that noise before was a coincidence."

"What noise?"

He shakes his head. "Not now." He spots the wife. She's half-hidden behind another ornamental curtain about twenty feet away. She's too large to be completely hidden. Even if she could have fit behind the curtain, the sobs would have given her away.

"Mrs. Bell?" Flower's voice walks the line between authoritarian and comforting. I wish I could do that. I'd probably just sound like a jackass.

She sniffles but tries to calm herself. She wipes her face on her sleeve and nods. Like she knows exactly what he wants.

She holds out her arms, wrists limp. "Go ahead and arrest me, Officer. But know that I didn't mean to do it!"

Whoa. What? Is this woman confessing to murder?

## 7

O f course, I don't get answers.

Because who always walks in at the most inconvenient moments?

That's right. Bennett.

This time he walks in with the D.A., some other investigators, and a group of medics in tow.

I don't even have time to appreciate his freshly-showered smell. Or time to notice how green the shitty lighting makes his eyes look. Or how his uniform clutches his biceps when he bends his arm.

I do have time to notice him ordering me to go sit down in a chair as if I was some freakin' citizen instead of law enforcement. I do have time to notice him getting chummy with the D.A. and the mayor and issuing orders to Flowers like he's a whipping boy.

Eventually, I realize Seena's sat down beside me. I feel like an idiot. I've been focused on pettiness toward Bennett. But Seena's eyes are still plastered on Becca. And his worries are way more serious.

"Hey, you don't have to tell me, but were you two—"

"Friends with benefits," He sighs. "I'm probably not supposed to tell you. She didn't want to date … yet." He sounds so lost.

I put an arm on his shoulder. I gesture vaguely at the medics on stage, who are trying to examine the bodies without touching them, since we don't know exactly what happened. All they've been able to declare for certain is that Becca's alive. They can see her breathing.

A pretty elf medic tries a spell, but a shimmer of purple sparks just ricochets back at her. It is not reassuring. "I'm sure those guys'll figure it out." Even *I* don't know if I believe myself.

"No talking," Flowers barks at me. "Not until everyone's given their statements."

We're all divided up, like elementary school. We're given paper and pens and thirty minutes to write down everything we heard or saw. Then we have to interview. Like written and oral exams. At least, that's what it feels like. Should I be nervous I'll say the wrong thing? I mean, the wife already confessed. I can see her over in the corner, wiping her blue nose with a wad of toilet paper someone handed her. The D.A. already spoke with her. So did Bennett and Flowers.

My testimony isn't that important, right?

But, then I worry that Flowers and Bennett are gonna look at it. That they might judge how much I observed and how many details I remembered. Investigators are supposed to notice things, right?

I try to be as objective as possible. As detailed as possible. Maybe they don't need to know about the notch in Tabby's ear or what Jackie was wearing. But heck, who knows? Maybe something I saw was a clue. But shouldn't I recognize it? Would it be bad if I wrote down something that was a clue and didn't realize it?

And what about what Flowers said about a noise? I didn't hear a noise. Do I need to get my hearing checked?

I sink my head into my fist. Damn. I didn't need all this drama. I need a nap. My eyelids flutter.

"Fox," Bennett's voice breaks me out of half-sleep.

"Wh-what?" I try to discreetly slide my hand to my lap and wipe off a tiny trail of drool on my thigh.

Seena's over by Flowers. I didn't even notice him leave.

Bennett rolls his eyes and tosses me a tablet. "Peppy Perk. Take it. You're gonna need to keep a stash of that on-hand from now on if you really want this job."

"Yes sir." I down the tablet and ignore the fizzy citrus flavor. Immediately, my heart rate picks up. "Are you ready to take my statement?"

Ben rolls his eyes. "Technically, yes. That's what I'm here for. But I've also managed to talk to the D.A. I reminded him how you helped with the high-profile Georgina Knight case. He said he'll let you observe the other interviews."

My eyebrows rise. "Really?"

He gives a half grin that makes my heart trip. *Tha-thump.* Is he feeling guilty about breaking up with me? Is he trying to be overly nice?

He should feel guilty. But … "What about Seena?"

Bennett looks surprised. "What about him?"

"Does he get to sit in?"

Bennett turns to look at him. I can already see the answer in his face. He didn't even ask for Seena.

"No special treatment!"

He grabs his hair in frustration. "Dammit, Ly. Work with me. You want experience. I'm trying to give you experience. You want a chance to prove yourself. I'm trying to give you that."

"But I want to earn it. I want to rise up because I'm good."

"You are good."

"Then let me prove it. Put us both on to observe and let me see if I can contribute more."

He closes his eyes and breathes through his teeth.

"Why do you have to be so difficult?"

"Fair is difficult?"

"Fine," he snaps. "Mostafavipour. Over here." Seena trots over. "You get to observe the interviews." Bennett levels a glare at me. "You will not participate."

I nod solemnly. So does Seena.

"Okay then," Bennett nods toward the wife. "We're gonna go over to her."

I cock my head. "I thought she already gave a statement."

"She did. But we have our recorder here. So everyone gets to give a statement again." Bennett gestures over to a golem with a big keyboard stamped into its stomach. It stomps stiffly over to stand by Bennett. If you ignore the glowing eyes, it's actually kind of friendly-looking.

"Seena, Lyon, meet ABC."

The golem nods and a little trickle of dust falls from its neck. I wonder how old the animated hunk of clay is. I decide to call him a boy. Because, it's easier and I can. Considering the D.A.'s office is too cheap to buy electronic recorders, I'm guessing this guy doesn't get many patch jobs.

We all turn and follow Bennett.

"Mrs. Bell," Bennett shakes her hand. "Now that we have an official recorder here, I'm going to need you to repeat your story. So that we have everything on the record."

Mrs. Bell nods and blows her nose.

"I just wanted Bernard to retire. I didn't think it was so bad. He worked and traveled all our lives. He never slowed down! That business. It was too much. If he had gotten this appointment, he would've been gone day and night."

ABC's fingers fly over his belly like he's playing the piano.

Bennett asks, "What did you do to try and ensure that your husband would retire?"

The question sets Mrs. Bell off again. She gives a huge sob blows her nose like a trumpet. "I ... I went to a witch doctor. I got a fainting spell put into my handkerchief. I tried it on myself first. I swear I didn't think it was that strong. I just didn't want them calling his name. I would never hurt Bernard."

Oh, yeah. I believe that. I wouldn't hurt my husband. Just publicly humiliate him on camera. This lady's a wreck.

I exchange a glance with Seena. He seems skeptical too.

"Name of the doc you saw?" Bennett shows no emotion. I immediately try to get my 'neutral' face on. Because, yeah, who's gonna confess to someone judgey? Dang. Five seconds in and I'm already making mistakes.

"Robert Dove."

"Ah, yeah. I know him," he replies. "You go with anyone? Get a receipt?"

"No. No. I paid gold. I—he did have me type my name on some kind of online contract. On the computer."

Seena's eyes light up a bit for the first time since we've been here. Great. That kind of boring crap is right up his alley. Dammit. I stare at the wife harder, as if that will make her confess something that's in my wheelhouse.

"Remember what day you went?"

"Last Tuesday. I'd just gone to the Baths." (Translation: she just went to the local gossip joint for lady bird-shifters. It advertises as a health club, but really it's a pool for them to splash in and a high ropes course where they perch and shoot the shit.)

Bennett tosses me a look that lets me know exactly what I'm gonna be doing tomorrow night. Dodging bird crap. "Okay, we'll follow up on that. Anything else you can think of? Bernard have any health issues?"

Mrs. Bell shakes her head no.

"And the handkerchief?"

"I gave it to him," she nods her head toward Flowers, who is approaching us with an embroidered hanky in a plastic evidence bag.

"Photo team's here," he tells us.

"Good. Want to take her and book her while I finish up here?" Bennett's question is not really a question. Flowers nods.

Bennett takes the hanky-in-a-bag and Flowers leads the murdering widow away.

I turn to my ex. "Well, that seems too easy."

He shrugs. "Eighty-five percent of murders ..."

"Yeah, yeah. Who's next?"

"Well, we need to take a break for photographs. I need to give the team some instructions. Just shadow me."

Seena and I trail behind Bennett. Our photo 'team' is one guy. Clearly, they spare no expense at the office. Ben stops near the photographer unloading his rig. He's a scrawny beta-looking dude in his fifties. Shorter than me.

"We need all angles. Might even ask you to go up and take some from the balcony looking down. It's probably nothing. But there's something wonky about this spell his wife bought. It makes touching his skin dangerous from what we can tell. So, I want to see what you might pick up on film."

Bennett moves on to the evidence-tagging team. But he's only a few feet away, so I stay put. I'd rather watch this photographer attach his lens than listen to Bennett tell some brownies what to bag up.

I admit, I geek out a little bit looking at the camera. It's a Nikon D5 XQD, and the guy puts a pretty sweet lens on it. I watch him pop off a few shots, then go to adjust the settings. My guess is he paid for that thing himself. No way the office ponied up the money.

Crap. Bennett's moving on.

I sigh and start to follow, but then the photographer lets out a curse.

"Shit!"

I turn to the photographer who's shaking the camera. I'm guessing mediocre wizard who had no choice but to turn to tech. Because if he was a real technophile, he'd never handle his precious princess like that. "Everything okay?"

"Think I've got a bad sensor," the guy replies.

"Really? That's a pretty new camera you have."

"I know. Like a brand-new." He tries a couple more shots and then sighs in frustration. "Shit on a stick. Now I've got to go all the way out to the car to get my second camera."

He sets down the expensive hunk of junk and stomps away.

I can't help myself. I mean it's a dream camera, even if this one is a lemon. I pick it up. I take some test shots of Bernard. I don't mess with the settings, because that's asking for a finger breaking in the photography world. But I totally see what the guy means. Every couple is shots there's a black spot on Bernard's neck. He's right. Must be a sensor on the fritz. Sorry girl, I pat the sleek camera body as I set it back down. That little girl's going back to the factory.

Oh damn! Bennett and Seena are talking to Max the Cat.

I hurry over.

Max's in the middle of speaking. "—don't see how you could think she was responsible. I've never seen such an idiot."

Bennett shoots me a little glare before turning back to Max. "Councilor I respect your opinion, but at this time I simply need your statement."

Max licks his paw and then cleans his ear haughtily. "You do know that I was on the board of Neuro-Magic? Back in the eighties, when they interviewed and investigated murderers. I have a pretty good idea of what makes up a murderer's psychology. And Mrs. Bell doesn't have it."

Bennett has a little more trouble keeping his neutral face at this point. "Just a statement please, Councilor."

Max gives an angry flick of his tail. "Fine. I was on stage. I was interviewed about potential candidates by that news bimbo. I watched the potentials while everyone else chatted. That pixie, the one with the strange pink fur. She's got a vicious streak in her. Most pixies do."

I completely agree with him, though Seena and Ben look annoyed. They, obviously, have never been dive-bombed by a pixie. You don't have to be a cat to get the hate on. Dive-bombing sucks.

Max continues, "Anyway, I could see her sizing up her competition. Speaking with Clo. They're related, you know. Clo is her great-great aunt or something."

"Yes, but what did you observe?"

"I'm telling you what I observed. Suspicious activity from the pixie."

Bennett grits his teeth. "Will you excuse me? I need a drink of water."

I grab Bennett's elbow before he can walk away. "Sir, there is one thing I was curious about."

That's it. He's totally gonna take me outside and strangle me after this. He specifically said no participation. When I'm dead, I want a giant jellybean gravestone, okay? Like huge.

Twelve feet. Okay. I take a deep calming breath. If these are gonna be my last moments, better make them count.

"Max, did you hear anything weird just before Bernard fell over the second time?"

The cat turns his blue eyes to me. "Yes. It was a whistle. Or a whiz. A whizzing whistle. Horribly high-pitched."

I nod. "Thank you. That is exactly what I wanted to know. You've been really helpful." I infuse my voice with extra gratitude. What? Cat's love to think they're superior. Why not milk it a little? If I can have a City Councilor think good of me, maybe Bennett won't be able to kill me after all.

"Cracked the case for you, did I?"

"You might have," I wink and walk away, leaving Seena and Bennett to trail after me.

"What was that?" Ben growls once we're out of earshot.

I look at Seena. "You heard that noise too, right? You were halfway across the room right before Bernard fell over."

"Yeah, why?"

"Did he describe the sound right? Did it sound like a whistle to you?"

"Yeah. Something scary though, like a moving whistle. Like a train. That doesn't make much sense. But something. It made my hair stand on end."

Bennett's growl is not the sexy kind. "Lyon, what's the point of this?"

"I didn't hear anything. But Honeycutt's bats swooped in. He ducked. Tabby and Max were both freaking out. Even Flowers mentioned hearing something."

"And?"

He doesn't get it.

"Why is it all the were-animals heard something, but I didn't?"

"Did the boobies react?" Ben asks.

This time, I don't even snicker. I'm too focused on the conversation. There's something here. I can feel it. But it's like sand in my hands. I don't quite know my own point yet.

Seena jumps in to help. "I don't know about sea boobies' hearing. But you're right. Gor didn't really react. Or most of the assistants. Jackie and her cameraman were still standing there, she was blabbing away."

"Okay. So we know there was a noise."

"A scary noise," I cut in.

"A scary noise," Bennett mocks me. "That only were-animals with sensitive hearing could hear. Why is that important?"

"I don't know yet."

Bennett lets out a snort. If he were in dragon form, smoke would be rolling off him right now. He'd be shooting sparks at me. If I wasn't already fried to a crisp. "Well, now that we've wasted time on this enlightening conversation, let's get back to work."

## 8

To my surprise, Bennett heads over to talk to the pixie.

"Why—"

"I'm not about to tick off one of our most important City Councilors by acting like I dismissed his theory. Especially not the one that has nine lives." Bennett replies. "We'll talk to her next, see what's up, and move on."

With a nod of respect, he steps in front of the pixie, who's hovering in place at head-height. "Miss Daisy, I'd like to take your statement on the record about what happened tonight. If you don't mind."

She nods and claps her hands to release a sprinkle of pixie dust, some of which she captures and smears on her throat to magnify her voice. I expect her to start talking, but she starts pulling at the neck of her dress like it's suffocating her. For a second, I wonder if we're about to have a third person collapse on us. But then I realize, she just stuck her hand down the front of her dress. And is rummaging around. OMG.

"You can call me Eudora, as long as you're okay with me chewing here," she rasps as she pulls out a tiny tin.

Bennett eyes slide left to right and he leans in conspiratorially. "It's fine by me 'til you get caught. Then I had nothing to do with it."

She laughs and it's a gruff, manly sound. Completely the opposite of what I was expecting.

She opens the tin and shoves something in her mouth. It takes me a second to realize its chewing tobacco.

"So, a statement you said?"

Next to her ABC creaks forward. He puts his head right next to where she's hovering on iridescent blue wings. I don't think life-infused clay men have the best hearing. But his fingers *tap-tap-tap* away at that belly.

Bennett gives her one of his killer smiles.

"Well I knew they were never gonna give it to me. Councilor. Told my squadron the same. Big waste of time for me to come from beyond the Veil. But politics, you know. Can't go shootin' Clo in the foot."

"Are you related to her?" Bennett tries to sound disinterested.

"Shoot, boy! I thought everyone knew that. She's my second cousin's step-grandmother. Might be once removed or something. Who knows with all those inbreeding fools beyond the Veil." Her eyes flicker to me and she raises her diamond encrusted brows.

"See you've got some fairy blood in you," Eudora gestures at the sapphire in my chin.

I nod but don't speak. First off, I'm not sure how Bennett would react if I broke the rules a second time. Secondly, she might've just insulted fairies, but it's one thing for a full fairy to insult her own kind and it's totally another thing for a part-Fae to insult fairies. Kinda like if I was gonna talk about your mother...

"Well I hope you have more sense than most of them," she spits. Literally.

I have to step aside, because she's got quite the range. Seena's not so lucky. Tobacco hits him right on the chest.

Bennett gives me a subtle nod. I'm guessing he wants me to get her back on track since she's engaging with me.

"I hope so ma'am," I respond. "Did you observe anything unusual today?"

"Besides that booby being a boob?" Her eyes twinkle.

I somewhat smother a snicker.

"Look all I know is that reporter was in our face blabbing on about how important this appointment was. And that goblin, Gor or Gory or whatever, was on his phone a couple times, answering questions for work, I guess. Something about consignment. And potions. That there seems like a shady business. Heard him tell some assistant to offer some hard-up Fae a quarter the value of his throwing stars. Highway robbery!" She pounds a tiny fist into her palm. "Criminal behavior, if you ask me. What with that—and that accusation being tossed out about his association with those Crypts hooligans—I wouldn't be surprised if he had something to do with all this. 'Just takes one step off the straight and narrow to start down a crooked path,' my mother always said."

"Did you see him do anything suspicious?" I follow up.

"Well, I wasn't really looking for it." For the first time, Eudora looks a little sheepish. "Let my guard down today. And look. I would ream one of my flyers if this happened to him!" She shakes her pink head. "Maybe I need to look at retirement. Did you know I was one of the first women ever to make captain?" She sighs. "522 years in. Some people might say that's long enough. But I'd always hope to die in battle, like Petal the Pickax or Vanquished Violet."

Bennett clears his throat. I can tell he's thoroughly annoyed by Miss Daisy's meandering thoughts.

"Other than Gor, did you see anyone else doing anything suspicious on stage? Did anyone bring any packages up or wave their fingers to do secret spell work?" Bennett is polite but clipped.

"I didn't hear much else. Clo was blabbing in my ear about the other City Councilors. Seems like they don't all get along."

"Why's that?" Bennett asks.

Eudora shakes her pink head. "Why else? Power. Idiots always become seduced by power. And they think being in the spotlight gives it to 'em. Real power comes from the tip end of your sword. That's what I always tell my squad. Don't get hung up on promotions. Don't get hung up on orders. All those can change. At the end of the day, the one with the power is the one that's still breathing. Closer you are to the top, less likely you are that's you. Top get the first chop." She grabs another pinch of snuff. "Clo seems to hate that vampire member. He seems a bit shady. She kept snapping at him about leaving during an important time. And he kept complaining about how long all this was taking. Of course, that's just tempers. But that cat, you know. Can't trust cats. Dunno what idiots elected him. I mean, look at what that orange one did. Jumping on a man like that. My squad woulda' ripped into her. She's a violent one, you can tell."

I have to work hard not to stiffen as she calls Tabby violent. Raspberry took the first swing. Tabby just grabbed him by the—don't argue in your head, Lyon. It shows on your face. Deep breath. Deep breath.

"Well, thank you." Bennett turns to leave and I take a step to follow him. That's why I almost slam into him when he turns back around. "Are you sure all the current City Councilors knew you were related to Clo?"

Eudora shrugs. "Like I said, I thought everyone knew when she tossed my name to the mayor as an option. Not like we used a cloaking spell to hide the family tree."

Bennett nods. "Please stay in town with her while we have this investigation open."

Eudora nods.

Seena salutes her as we leave.

Eudora just spits another wad at him and he has to duck as we walk away.

"Well, she's off her rocker," Seena mumbles once we're out of earshot.

"She's actually the most pleasant pixie I've ever met," I respond.

"Don't think I need to meet anymore then," he grins at me.

"Probably not. They tend to be terrors. I think age has mellowed her."

"Mellowed her mind," Bennett shoots back.

I shrug. What he says is true.

"We dodged a bullet with her nearly being the appointee," Bennett looks at ABC. "Strike that from the record."

ABC frantically hits backspace.

"In fact, we're gonna take a quick break. Go over and help out Teri down there. Food's here." Bennett nods toward a delivery donkey with a pack on its back.

Yum! I'm thrilled until I realize that the delivery is sushi. Leave it up to a tiger-shifter to order expensive fishy crap. What was he thinking? My tummy protests. I sigh. Oh well. At least Town Hall has vending machines.

I go grab some peanut M&Ms and a candy bar. I don't know why vending machines don't carry jellybeans. It's like their deliciousness is a hidden secret only I know. Sad. Until I go to the store and clean out every bag they have! (Muhahhaha —an evil villain laugh is always necessary when your arms are full of *all* the jellybeans.)

Seena is also not a fan of the fish food. He's stuck plowing through the edamame.

A little ways away, Bennett is tossing sushi disks down his throat. I sit on a chair next to him and nudge his foot with mine. What? That's not flirting is it? It's just a friendly hello. To a hot supervisor.

"Flowers is never allowed to order takeout again," I declare.

"Technically, his assistant did it."

"Don't care. Only you like this crud," I say.

"Yeah, well the mayor should never be allowed to nominate candidates again," he confides in a low voice.

"She didn't really think she was gonna get it," I whisper back.

"But look at Bernard." Our gazes drift to the body, which still can't be removed because the highly trained and oh-so-magically-competent medical team can't figure out what's wrong with him or Becca. What's it been, three hours? Thirty spells? Still no clue. Not inspiring a lotta confidence, guys.

"I'm looking."

"He was an idiot, too."

I shrug. "Maybe Gor was the choice all along and the mayor had to just put butts in the seats to make it look fair."

Bennett turns to me. "How can you shrug off the mayor being unfair about the most important post in town, but you ride my ass about letting pony-boy tag along?"

I meet his gaze head on. Oh no you don't, Mr. French. I stare into his eyes and will myself not to get lost in the sea of green. What the hell is it with him and talking about everything? Focus on work. Stay on work. Don't make me cry at work. It's not hard. He wants to play it like that. Fine. I'll play it like that. Suck it up, Ly. Straight delivery. Hit him where it hurts. "Easy. I hold the potential father of my future children to a higher standard."

He chokes. "What?" His face goes through fifty shades of freaked out. The expressions are so exaggerated he looks like a mime. I consider pulling out my camera.

"Oh, I got you good. You freaked!"

He shakes his head, still coughing. "Don't ever do that again."

"Bennett, don't you wanna be my baby-daddy?" I bat my eyes.

"Not fair. We have not had this conversation."

I don't give a shit about fair. Right now, I'm just glad the tears have been swallowed back into the abyss. Work. I need more work. I let my gaze wander around the room. It looks like ABC and another investigator are talking with Tabby and Sarah Snow. "Fine. I'll stop. But only because I don't want you embarrassing yourself any more in front of the mayor."

Bennett rolls his eyes. "Thank you, Ms. Fox."

I stand.

He grabs my hand and interlaces our fingers.

"Don't. People will see."

"I don't care."

"I do."

Bennett's eyes turn dark. He leans forward. And even though I'm standing and he's still sitting, the authority rolling off of him is palpable. "Since you wanted to bring up bearing my children, I thought I'd let you know... I have a ring. Ready and waiting."

My heart stops. My cheeks heat. What the mother eff? Is he serious?

This time, he smirks. "Gotcha."

I storm off. Jerk-face.

## 9

I head over to Tabby and Mrs. Snow.

Scaring Bennett was fun. He got me back. But oh, he'll get his.

I sigh. He came way too close to talking about real stuff. I can tell when he gets that look in his eyes. He did it the first time we broke up, too. He's weird. I mean, who talks to their ex after a breakup about the breakup? Just now he wanted to psychoanalyze why I hold him to a higher standard. Geez. We have to work together, but there's no way I want to air all this out at a murder scene. I mean, shouldn't he be focused on that? We should definitely be focused on that, right?

I rub my eyebrows to stave off a migraine. Compared to Bennett, Luke's sweet attention is so uncomplicated. And he invited me on a date. Kinda. To help me practice spells.

That's a date, right? Shit. Now I feel guilty for flirt-teasing Bennett. I'm gonna have to tell JR I can't help with wedding sweatshop tonight. Even with Peppy Perk, I'm clearly a danger to society. And hearts. (My own included.) I have a firm no-reckless heartbreaking policy. So… yeah. Sleep. And work.

I walk past Becca's stiff form. The medics have a green haze swirling around her now, trying out yet another tentative cure. Yes. Focus. See? This is what I mean. I need to help Becca. So that she can wake up and we can execute our Halloween plans for Seena. That's four nights away.

I have to pass the crusty photographer on my way to my friends. I stop when he starts shaking his camera like a maniac.

"Are you freaking kidding me?" he mutters.

"Whoa. What's up? Can I help?"

He turns to me, about to snarl, but then his lip gives an extra twist and I worry he might cry. Awkward. "Both of my cameras are broken."

"Can I take a look?" I gently relieve the pretty black camera body from his death grip. I take a couple test shots. I see nothing wrong. But I don't want to make Mr. Mental-Instability worse, so I casually ask, "What seems to be the problem?"

"Pixelation. The other camera, my newer one, has it too. I think my grandmother's cursed me. That witch. She never wanted me to take this job in the first place. But to ruin two cameras ... Do you know how much that costs?"

I take another test shot. "I'm not seeing pixelation."

The photog raises his eyebrows. "Maybe it is a curse then. On me. You mean my cameras aren't broken?"

I aim a test shot at the bodies. And there it is. Dammit. A dark spot.

"Shoot."

"Oh man! You see it?"

"Yeah." I take a few steps and try another test shot, zooming in on Bennett. No spots. Turn back to the bodies. *Click.* A spot. "Wait."

I take another few steps. *Click.* Check the on-screen image. A spot. But the spot is moving around. Bad pixels don't move. They create a dead spot on the screen. But I'm moving, taking shots in different places. Always aiming at the bodies but different angles. The spot shows up on Raspberry's neck, no matter where I seem to stand.

I pause, holding up a hand to stop the camera guy who's come to take back his equipment. His other rig showed pixelation too. Two cameras with the same issue? It can't be a coincidence. But what can it mean?

Just then—with the perfect timing of real-life coincidence that somehow manages to seem impossible—Tabby hollers at her investigator.

"I bet this is all gonna be some massive cover up!"

I turn to look at her, holding the camera overhead so the photo-wizard can't easily grab it back. (Thank goodness he's so short.) A cover up.

Eudora flutters by and suddenly my brain's on overdrive. Something she said ... Cover up. Cloaking spell. That's it!

"Give that back!" Photo-wiz stomps his foot.

"Oh, keep your shirt on. I'm about to save you from looking like a fool." I start adjusting settings on his camera. I turn the frame rate up to 240 per second. I turn back to Bernard the booby. I zoom. And start taking rapid-fire photos of his neck. There! And there! Every eight frames or so I see something. An outline or something. I go to the menu and delete the 'normal' frames. I start flipping through the messed up photos. Faster. And faster. Like those flip-book comics they used to make us draw in third grade. And I see it. A tube. Or a vial. Raspberry's got something sticking out of his neck.

"Shut the front door!" I did it! I figured out a clue! Or found evidence. Or whatever. But I did it! I could do a happy dance. I wink at the pouting photo-wizard before I yell, "Bennett!"

"What are you doing?"

"I think your pixel is actually the murder weapon," I state as Bennett hurries over.

Wiz grabs the camera from me and so my chance to ogle Bennett as he jogs over is ruined. But still. "Good news—"

"I found the murder weapon!" Wiz interjects.

My jaw drops. Literally drops. That little wimpy biotch is trying to steal my thunder. "You did not. I figured it out!"

"No. You just stole my camera to try to take credit!"

I press my lips together so hard my teeth are digging into them. I really want to smack this little shithead into next week. But that won't help. And Honeycutt's heading our way.

I turn to Bennett, fire in my eyes. He does one of those crappy 'let's all calm down' hand gestures. I want to smack him.

"I'm more interested in what was found than who found it right now," he gestures for the camera, which wimpy photo-wizard gives him.

Bennett looks at the preview screen. "What am I looking at?"

"See that thing in his neck? I think it killed him," Wiz says.

"If you flip through several photos, pressing that little arrow button, you'll see 'that thing' is actually a tube or a vial or something. It's stuck in his neck," I add. "The first shot shows the part of it right near the neck and if you flip quickly, you can kind of get an idea of the whole thing."

Bennett follows my instructions and swears under his breath. "That's it."

Honeycutt interjects. "You've found the murder weapon?"

I catch a whiff of hairspray. I turn and see Jackie Hanna edging closer. Oh no you don't.

"Bennett, press," I whisper. I jerk my head at the nymph.

"Neo, please escort Ms. Hanna to a seat," Bennett calls out. "Across the room."

Jackie glares daggers at me as an officer with a lizard tail hauls her off.

Honeycutt waits patiently until she's gone. "Be careful with that one. She's relentless."

"Yes, sir."

"So, found the weapon?" Honeycutt repeats his earlier question.

"Looks like it sir," Bennett replies. "Syringe to the neck. Must be poison. Or a potion."

Honeycutt, though he's not technically supposed to be allowed to see the inner workings of a pending investigation, leans forward and peers over Bennett's shoulder. I guess he's exercising executive privilege or something. I just know enough to keep my big mouth shut.

"And why can we see it on camera?"

Bennett turns to me and Wiz. I give it a second, to see if Wiz will jump on the answer. Of course he doesn't. Because he doesn't know what I did. I put the little wizard in his place with my eyes and open my mouth. "I think the weapon is under a cloaking spell, sir. But I think it's only set to work at normal vision levels. The human eye sees around twenty-four distinct images every second. Video can be about thirty to sixty frames per second so it looks nice and smooth. I set the camera to two-hundred forty frames per second. That's how we saw this."

Bennett flips through the photos again, Honeycutt leaning over his shoulder.

"That looks like a dart," Honeycutt says. "A hunting dart."

Bennett's eyes flick to mine. "Mr. Mayor, are you familiar with hunting darts?"

Honeycutt bristles. "If you're implying—"

"No sir. But the sound you claimed you heard before Mr. Bell fell over. Did it sound like a hunting dart?"

Honeycutt's eyes widen. "I haven't been for a few years. You might want to ask Giancarlo." He jerks his horns toward the vampire Councilor, who's lounging onstage, looking annoyed. "He's an avid hunter. But yes, I'd say it did."

"I didn't hear it. So I'm guessing the same rule applies to cloaking the sound," I toss out. The conversation with Max the Cat about sound takes on new meaning. "Whoever set this spell didn't account for sight or hearing above normal levels."

"So they were lazy," Bennett concludes.

"Or stupid." I shrug.

"Either way, that should make them easy to catch." The mayor gives Bennett a congratulatory smack on the back. "Nice work." Then he strolls off.

Wiz looks at Bennett. "Can I have my camera back?"

"No. I'm putting it into evidence."

I'm not sure if Bennett really needs the camera or if he's just being petty for my sake. I kind of hope it's the latter. His eyes are saying it's the latter. Triumph and lust mingle in his gaze.

We share a hot, intense, elated moment. Yes, Mr. French. I'm good at this. So good you want to take me back to your place and celebrate. His eyes shout, 'Hell yes! I want to celebrate until you scream!'

"We're still broken up," I whisper. Because? I don't know why. Because my stupid mouth is hemorrhaging words, okay? I'm an idiot. Pride. The worst emotion ever— and I've got a lot of it—that right now I want to rip to shreds so that Ben can go to work ripping my clothing to shreds. Holy hell. I did not think working together would be so hot. Like not at all. I'm just as stupid as this killer.

Bennett's eyes crinkle as he smiles at me. I think he can sense my internal monologue. "At this rate, not for long. Good work, Fox. Keep it up."

ennett speaks with the medical team about the dart in Bernard's neck. They instantly light up and start discussing potential antidotes. The relief of at least narrowing down the cause of death is palpable.

"A dart means liquid. There are only fifty-seven liquid potions or poisons known to kill shifters," a brunette elf medic states. She tucks a strand of hair behind her pointed ear. Long and lithe, she looks more like a ballerina than a medical examiner. "Of those, only twenty-five are single-dose lethal. But, if we can extract the dart and get it to the lab, hopefully we can get enough residue to test for all of those. Thank you." She places a graceful hand on Ben's forearm. My eyes are drawn like magnets. Or lasers. The kind that burn the hands off stupid little—I stiffen when

Bennett smiles. At her or at my response, I'm not sure. But I do not like it.

"Here, I can show you where the dart is," I take a deep breath, tap the elf on the shoulder, and lead her toward the body. I want to get her back to the lab and away from Bennett ASAP. I show her where the dart seems to be placed, on the left side of Raspberry's neck. She tosses on some blue gloves, then grabs some crystal magic-resistant tongs and gets to work.

I step back to watch her.

"Jealous?" Bennett whispers in my ear.

"Just trying to be helpful," I make my voice sweet and innocent.

Damn. He caught me. I can't be possessive. Stupid. Stupid. We aren't together. He made it official the other day. A hot moment during a case doesn't mean I'm not still right. I need some separation. To learn how to do this myself. To make my own way. I'm not into hand-holding and nepotism. None of that makes me feel much better when I watch the elf delicately extract the dart and give a gorgeous nerdy grin to Bennett. He gives a thumbs up.

I turn away. I have to get over him. I try to cheer myself up. I do have a semi-date coming up. A study date. Yeah. I'm calling it that. Like some stupid high schooler.

I spot Tabby and Sarah Snow and wave at them, trying to escape Bennett's speculative gaze at the side of my face.

Sarah eagerly waves back. Tabby's still a cat, but she twitches her tail, so I take that as a hello. (Note to self: I need to tell Sarah to tamp down on her excitement at murder scenes. It could be taken the wrong way.)

Bennett summons Seena and tells the pair of us to shadow him. He fills Seena in on the dart discovery as we head toward Giancarlo Russo, who's lounging in a chair stage left. Jackie Hanna's sitting next to him and sliding her hand along his arm.

I catch the last couple words she says, "…just a little comment on the record."

Mr. Russo looks relieved to see our group and quickly stands.

Bennett politely makes Jackie get lost while I linger in the background, a few steps behind. Not avoiding Bennett. Avoiding Mr. Russo. Vamps are too much like candy for me. Delicious. Endlessly tempting. I'm just being professional. Not a coward. Or an idiot who's tempted to beg the boss that just terminated our relationship to reconsider. I am absolutely neither of those. Right.

Mr. Russo runs a hand through his silver flecked hair, catching my attention. I swallow a sigh. Maybe this is what I need. A beautiful distraction. But then comes that Italian accent.

"How can I be of a'service?"

A million dirty responses immediately jump to mind. And like *that*, depressed self-pity—gone. Poof. If it's that easy, maybe I need some recordings of Giancarlo's public speeches. You know, for mental health purposes.

"You like hunting, right?"

"Yes. It is a hobby."

"Which hunt club do you belong to?"

"Benne Notte."

"And you go regularly? Enough to recognize the sound of a dart gun?"

Giancarlo's eyes widen a bit as he sees where Ben is going.

"Did the noise just prior to Mr. Bell's collapse sound like a dart gun to you?" Bennett asks.

Giancarlo raises his eyebrows. "Now that you mention … perhaps yes. You think this was what killed him?"

Bennett doesn't answer. "You previously spoke about your plans for later today. You were going hunting, right?"

Giancarlo's eyes narrow. "I believe this is where I invoke my rights, yes? To an attorney? Silence? Those things?"

This could be bad. Very bad. We do not want to get on the wrong side of the City Council. They make the laws. They set our budget. We *just* got a coffee machine. Because, apparently, the government doesn't like to pay for frills. You know, like stimulants to keep the day shift people awake through their god-awful hours. Our machine's been named. Gloria. Because she's glorious. Before that, everyone had to order Broomer delivery. Do you know how hard it is to get a full cup of coffee delivered by a witch zooming around on a broom? The look in Giancarlo's eyes says that Gloria's in danger.

Seena and I share a scared glance.

My eyes flick back to Bennett. I don't think I breathe as I wait for him to speak.

Bennett's face is as calm as a lake. "I would never accuse you, sir," Bennett responds. "You were onstage the entire time."

Giancarlo nods in agreement. But I think he's taking the fifth pretty seriously.

"What I'm interested in knowing is who on your staff might have had access to your weapons."

Giancarlo raises an eyebrow. "Yes. I am interested in this as well. All the same, I would prefer to have my attorney present. I need a phone call."

"You aren't being detained, Sir. You're free to call whomever you please. Note that my team has set up spelled surveillance of the building as this is a murder investigation. If you make a call, you are required to inform the other party of this fact before you speak to them."

Mr. Russo gives a brief nod.

Bennett leads us to the hall outside the main room. "That was helpful."

"What?" I peer back at the vampire. "He didn't tell us anything."

"He seemed worried he might say the wrong thing," Bennett replies. "Seena, Lyon, please begin a search of the premises. Lyon, show Seena how to use the camera. Based on the angle that dart penetrated, it was a downward shot. My investigators already did a preliminary sweep of the balcony. Didn't find a weapon. Only a camera clipped to the railing from that idiot news team. Search again. I'm guessing the weapon's got the cloaking spell too."

I nod.

Seena interjects. "Excuse me, sir. Why'd you warn Mr. Russo about the spelled surveillance?"

"California is a dual-party consent state. Tres Lunas has its own laws. Too many immortals gaming the system. We're single-party. But since Russo's not the one doing the recording, he could take out a civil suit against us if I didn't tell him. Any place someone might have an expectation of privacy, better to let them know."

"Oh."

He waves us toward the staircase. I grab the two cameras my friend Wiz had to leave behind and we head up. Seena slides his eyes sideways toward me. "So… the vampire or the boss, huh?"

"What's the Persian phrase for shut your pie-hole?"

"Khafeh sho."

"Yeah. That." I bitch-slap him with my eyes.

But he just laughs. "I'm glad you figured out the murder weapon."

"Medics seemed like they were confident they could figure out the poison or whatever," I respond, thinking Seena's glad about Becca.

His response is not what I expect at all. "But you know *I'm* gonna catch the murderer." He says it like it's a fact of life. A foregone conclusion. Nerdy analyst just smacked me with a challenge.

I raise an eyebrow. "Did you just throw down, pony boy?"

"Bet your ass I did." He winks behind his glasses as we finish ascending the stairs.

I fix the speed settings and hand him a camera. "What dya' wanna bet?"

Seena thinks for a minute. "I win, then there will be no glitter pony Halloween costume."

"And if I win?"

"I'll let you dye my hair pink."

Oh man. It's on.

We spit on our hands and slap each other's cheeks. (Leftover dueling gesture. From the gory glory days of shifter fights for territory.) The challenge is official. No backing down.

"I take left, you take right?" I try to keep a straight face. I'm suddenly super-glad that Bennett didn't happen to mention to Seena that Bernard was shot on his left side.

Seena sees right through me and dashes over to the left.

"Khafeh sho!"

"Improper use!" He calls over his shoulder.

"Yeah, well I hate you!" I grumble. Then I start shooting the place up—with my camera. The balcony overlooks the mayor's speech podium perfectly. Too bad there aren't any security footage spells up here. Would've made our lives easier. It woulda' been wham, bam, case closed m'am. But … then I'd be out of a job instead of waving my hand through space looking for an invisible gun and taking pictures trying to see black specks and determine if they're ants, dirt on the carpet, or something more sinister.

As expected, Seena's the one to find the weapon. An army of brownies tumble over themselves as they come up the stairs to collect it and take it for fingerprinting. Brownies are about two feet tall, with pug noses. So it basically looks like Bennett's sent a wild pack of children to bag evidence. I have to smother a grin. Because no self-respecting brownie likes to be called cute.

Also as Bennett expected, Giancarlo confirms it's his gun once he sees the photos. Of course, he claims both he and his assistant had access to the gun case this evening. But his attorney, a man roughly the size of a semi-truck wearing a zebra-print suit, does one of those 'cut it out' throat slash gestures.

"Do you think we could open your gun case to confirm, sir?" Bennett asks politely, ignoring the Mac-truck in the suit.

The vamp looks at his lawyer for approval before nodding and leading us backstage. We go down a long hall and turn right. His office is lush. Copper-colored velvet drapes. He obviously had his claw-footed desk brought in. Two mirrors. (I don't know why he has those either.) A vase that looks like it's worth more than my apartment holds white roses. In the corner, there's a rolling suitcase, a locked metal ammo container, and a gun case.

Giancarlo pulls the gun case onto his desk and reaches for a hidden inner pocket. His eyes cloud over for a moment. He pats another pocket.

"Is there something wrong?" Bennett has the balls to ask.

"No, no. Here it is. Justa' forgot which pocket," he pulls out the key and unlocks the gun case.

His attorney takes a step closer to Giancarlo and reminds him, "You don't have to do this."

"It's alright, Charles. I'm innocent," the vamp throws open the gun case.

I have to lean around Bennett to peer inside. The case is empty.

Bennett sighs. "I'm going to need to collect this case as evidence. And I'm going to need to meet you at the station in twenty for some more questions."

"Am I under arrest?"

"Not yet, Mr. Russo. But it doesn't look good." Bennett rubs his forehead.

The vamps lips thin to a tight line, but he gives a curt nod.

Ben snaps on some gloves and picks up the case. "See you there."

I follow Bennett into the hall. Once I'm fairly sure we won't be overheard, I ask, "Why are you letting him go in on his own?"

For the first time in hours, Bennett's eyes twinkle in amusement. "Fox, you should have figured that out already. I'm giving his lawyer a chance to speak with him."

"And that's good for the case, why?"

His grin just stretches farther. He pulls an earbud from his ear and hands it to me.

I toss it in my ear and hear Charles, the stripe-y semi truck.

"Is there anything I need to know about?"

"No."

"You had nothing to do with this?"

"No."

"How did they get access to your gun?"

"That, I would like to know. I dunno. Maybe my assistant? Secretary? She has keys also. This is what disturbs me most."

"Someone setting you up?"

"That would be their mistake." Giancarlo's voice is eerily calm for someone who thinks he might have been set up for murder. Of course, as a vamp, maybe this isn't his first rodeo. Most of the immortals in town have some kind of experience with the dark side. It's why murder doesn't carry a life sentence here.

"You need me to look into it?"

"No. I know someone."

"It better not be the someone I'm thinking of."

"No. I know someone who can do the job for me."

"Who?"

"The dragon has a lie machine at the station, no? Let him test them first."

"You think that thing works?"

"I have full confidence that if you and I say it works, my secretary and blockhead assistant will believe it. You will bring them, yes?"

"Sure."

"I'll meet you there."

"Wait. Do you want me to talk to ... *her?*"

"Hush! Did you forget where you are? There is recording. Even now. Especially now. You are supposed to be award-winning lawyer, no? Don't tell me all those stars on your website mean nothing. Go."

The conversation ends.

"Well, shit," Bennett curses.

"Zahré mar!" I agree, glad for once that Seena's vocab lesson can apply in context.

"What?"

"Never mind. Why are you upset?"

"It sounded like the lawyer was gonna mention Cookie. The Crypts."

"You got all that from the word 'her?'" I raise an eyebrow.

Bennett shrugs. "Maybe. Got cut off too early to tell. But ties between the leader of the Crypts and a City Councilor. That would be bad."

"Yes, well unless Cookie Garcia legally changes her name to 'her' I think you'll have a hard time proving who they were talking about. Besides, what does any of that have to do with Bernard Bell falling over dead?"

"Nothing. Yet."

Bennett takes off with Giancarlo's assistant and secretary to question the 'real' suspects.

Seena and I get stuck shadowing Flowers, who questions the remaining witnesses. For the next six hours. This includes Tabby and Sarah. Who absolutely should never *ever* be present at a murder scene again. Ever.

"Oh my goodness! That wife was a piece of work, wasn't she? I can't believe she did it!" Sarah exclaims.

Tabby has gone to the bathroom and shifted. She wears a spare set of workout clothes (from one of the female shifter investigators) and is practically swimming in the t-shirt. "Birds are mostly evil creatures." She shrugs, as if that's a statement of fact.

To my surprise, Sarah nods in agreement. "I've been to that ole' bath a' theirs. Those biddies have their beaks stuck up so high, they'll be drowning in a rainstorm."

For Sarah to say it, it must be true.

Flowers simply sighs. He's not as tactful as Bennett about keeping witnesses on point. "Did you see anything *actually* related to the murder?"

"Other than her attempt to murder me with her purse?" Tabby pushes her thick glasses up her nose until her eyes look twice their normal size. "I didn't hear anyone ask me yet if I want to press charges, by the way. The answer is yes."

Crap.

Flowers leaves me filling out paperwork for Tabby's charges, which I'm pretty sure the D.A. is just gonna drop. But there's no way I'm going to argue with her. Especially not once Max the Cat casually strolls over and listens in.

He washes an ear as I fill out ancient triplicate forms with Tabby's information. I do a double-take when she tells me her age, but then she lets me know she's on her sixth life. So, yeah. Four hundred twenty years isn't so crazy.

"So, Councilor," Sarah Snow looks delighted at the high-ranking company. "I'm sure that this isn't the most scandalous thing you've ever seen, but I'm surely gonna have daymares when I go to bed."

"Oh, I dunno," Max comments. "The swamp-thing protests back in the eighties were pretty terrible. Slime everywhere. But social media is turning this into a big to-do."

I look at him. "Wait. How are you getting social media updates?"

He rolls his eyes at me and his whiskers twitch in disdain. "Earbuds."

"You had earbuds in during a televised announcement?" I would have thought the announcement of a new City Council member would rank work higher than that.

But Tabby laughs. "Yarn Cup fan?"

"Of course."

"What team are you rooting for?"

"Croatia."

"Those cats don't stand a chance. Not with what France pays to recruit."

"France is insane. Anyone can unroll a ball of yarn." Max snaps.

"I heard they get a lifetime supply of M&Ms."

"M&M's?" Sarah asks.

"Mice & Men. All organic. Posh cat food," Tabby waves a hand.

"Are men an ingredient?"

I interrupt, because I see this conversation is quickly going off the rails. "Sorry. But what was it about social media and this murder?"

Max turns his eyes to me and his pupils narrow. "Oh, it's everywhere. There are already a hundred different suspects. And a cool name too. 'The City Council Killer.'" He tosses on a dramatic tone for effect.

Sarah raises her hand to her heart. "Now that sounds like a serial killer name."

"Yup. That's what the press is hinting at. That *we're next.*"

Tabby and Sarah's eyes pop in horror. Mine pop for a different reason.

I look over at Jackie, who's innocently tapping away at her phone. Just like twenty other people around the room.

"Scat!" Bennett didn't deal with the press before he left. I stand up. "One sec, guys. I'll be back."

I jog over to Jackie and grab her phone. "Excuse me. I think this might be evidence. FLORES!" I bellow.

He comes over and I show him Jackie's Frightbook posts, which have already gone viral. Of course, she's the one who's come up with the name City Council Killer and insinuated this might be the work of a serial killer.

Flores utters some choice words before radioing Bennett.

Jackie gets put in 'time out' in the corner without her phone as we wait for our fearless leader to return and feed a line of B.S. to the press to end this craziness.

I go back to finish Tabby's paperwork and interrupt a full-on argument between Tabby and Max over Yarn Cup players.

"He's the best we've seen since 1873! He's like Grotowski reincarnate!"

"He's not! He's got a total tell! His tail twitches left each time he—"

"Hi! Friendly D.A. investigator returning to do her job. We were in the middle of filing assault charges, right?"

"Attempted murder," Tabby corrects me. "You did put attempted murder right?"

"Well, the D.A. will have to decide whether a purse is considered a deadly weapon—"

"Oh, it is," Max says darkly.

I do not wanna know. I just add 'attempted murder' to the list and hope this doesn't end up on JR's desk.

Ten minutes and two more interrupted Yarn Cup arguments later, Bennett arrives.

Immediately, Tabby stops to swoon. "Dragon man's back."

Sarah tosses an arm around my shoulders. "She's not interested. She's going out with sweet Luke now."

"Luke? Luke Hawkins?" Max asks as Bennett walks up.

"Yes, he asked her out just before the press conference started. It was so sweet," Sarah responds.

I feel a hand on my shoulder and look up. A very angry Bennett French stares down at me. A thread of panic weaves through my stomach. Did he hear that bit about Luke asking me out?

His eyes burn into mine. I'm pretty sure the answer is yes.

"Luke Hawkins was here?"

Sarah does not pick up on the tension, though Max and and Tabby's necks twist to face me, then Bennett, then look back again. Like they're watching the ball of wool swivel between players in the Yarn Cup.

I can see the flames in Bennett's eyes. My mouth dries out. I can't answer.

"Yes, he dropped Tabby and I off before he had to scoot on down to work," Sarah answers.

"Really?" Ben raises his eyebrows. His tone is conversational but his eyes … His eyes burn a hole through me. I do not want to be alone in a room with him right now.

"Excuse us," Ben grabs my upper arm and hauls me to a deserted hall.

"What the fuck!?" he snarls.

I shrink back.

"Did you break it off with me so you could get together with him?"

"No!" That is such B.S. "I didn't want to break up with you at all! I just wanted space."

He clenches his fists and forces himself to take a deep breath. "What the hell, Lyon? Explain. Please."

"He just offered to help me with my powers. I suck. Okay? I suck. I'm bottom of the class. Like *every* day. And I just—"

"Why didn't you ask me for help?" He's gone soft. Gentle. His hand touches my shoulder.

"Because nothing's changed. It's like I said. I want to see if I'm good at this."

"You were amazing today."

I shake my head. "That's a one-off. I need to do it."

His voice hardens. "So, you'll let him help you but not me?"

"You broke up with me!"

"I did not!"

"Yes," I can't hide the tremor in my voice any longer. "When you came to the gym the other day. You said six months was …" I have trouble even saying the words. It makes my chest hurt. Get tight. Like really tight. Like tourniquet cutting off the blood flow tight. My hands come up. I curl in on myself. I can't help it. It's physical pain so bad my body just reacts. I swallow a sob.

"God, Ly. No. I didn't mean that. I didn't mean … you've thought this for days?"

I manage a nod.

"You didn't fight me over it."

I shake my head. "It wouldn't be fair. To make you wait."

His eyes are full of tears. I think. Mine are so full of tears it's hard to tell. Everything's blurry.

Silence stretches between us. Long and jagged, like a sword, cutting through whatever connection we've had.

He doesn't argue. I half want him to argue, like he has been. To bug me about it. To give me some sign that we're getting back together. He doesn't.

Finally, he pinches the bridge of his nose between his fingers. "Luke Hawkins was here." His tone is dead, matter of fact.

I nod.

"He was here shortly before the murder. But left before it happened."

I nod again.

"So he had opportunity."

My head jerks up. But before I can say anything, Bennett's gone.

Did he just accuse Luke of murder?

## 12

Does it matter that I worked until 7:30 in the frickin' morning?

Not to JR, who's standing inside my apartment and yanks open my door when I drag my exhausted butt home.

Does she care that I have to be at the Academy at five p.m.? She does not.

Why?

"My cousin just added a theme to her wedding. A theme, Lyon!" She looks ready to punch me. If it means she'll let me pass out, I'm tempted to let her.

I eye her dully, trying not to doze where I stand. "What's the theme?"

"Lovebirds. Some stupid celebrity in L.A. had a theme wedding. And she just has to have the same. Now, we have to come up with decorations with white feathers and twinkle lights and branches."

I nod as I fumble with my key. I think there must be a disconnect between my ears and my brain right now because I say, "That's nice."

"Nice! Nice! How the hell am I supposed to change the decorations that fast?"

"Yoo-hoo? Is that you JR?" Mrs. Snow comes up the stairs. Her hair is in the kind of pink foam curlers I haven't seen in a decade. She's wearing a flower-patterned robe.

JR bites her lip, "I'm so sorry I woke you up."

Mrs. Snow waves a hand dismissively. "Like I could sleep with all that chaos last night. It's just been on repeat in my brain."

"Chaos?"

"Oh, honey, didn't Lyon tell you? Tabby and I were there for the murder!" She says this like she was there for the birth of a child, or some other triumphant event. She sweeps past me and turns on the lights in my living room. She takes a seat on my purple velvet couch. "Got any tea?"

So, I guess this means I'm not getting to sleep any time soon. I rub a hand over my face and start searching my cabinets while JR and Mrs. Snow prattle on. I find the tea, get the water on the stove, and then lean my forehead against the fridge for just a sec ...

The whistle of the tea kettle startles me awake and I bonk my head against the fridge.

"Crab-cakes!"

I rub my forehead as I get out cups and pour water into them, giving each woman a teabag. Mrs. Snow gets some orange-cranberry nastiness and JR gets lavender. I hope it calms her down, but from the pitch of her voice, that's gonna take a while.

"Insane! I tell you!"

"Oh sweetie, I wish I had that pause potion for you. But I had to use it today to save that girl's life," Mrs. Snow's voice swells with self-importance as I hand her teacup over. "I'll try and get another one brewed to give you more time, but I just don't know if it'll be done before you need it. Some of those ingredients are on backorder."

JR sighs and sinks into her chair, "Thanks anyway."

"But I do have some suggestions. First off, centerpieces. We just take those flowers we already planned and toss a white birdcage over them. Easy-peasy. Change that cookie order from Wendel's so that those are bird-shaped sugar cookies. For some atmosphere, you can have some different wings for the guests to try on and take photos in. Kind of a half-bird shifter idea. Might look more like those human angels, but still, not too bad right? The girls and I could sew a couple a' those for you."

JR is tearing up. She grabs Mrs. Snow's hand. "I don't know what I'd do without you. You're a genius."

Mrs. Snow shakes her head, but she blushes and pats JR's hand in thanks before she takes a sip of tea. "As for the room itself, I once attended a party with little origami birds suspended from the ceiling. I think you could order those online real easy from some human store."

"I'll go grab my laptop. It's in my bedroom," I offer the sole help I can.

After wading through the laundry and naughty paperbacks strewn across my floor, I find my laptop. But the battery is dead. I toss it on the charger. I figure it will only need a few minutes ... I sit next to it on the bed.

Next thing I know, the sun is shining on my face. JR, that evil hag, has pulled up my blinds.

"Nooky!" I shield my eyes with my arms.

"Good morning, Princess."

I hiss, turning away from the light. "What time is it?"

"Nine. We let you sleep as long as possible. But, I'm leaving, and I figured you'd want to be able to lock your door."

"What happened to your key?" I grumble into my sheets.

"It's enchanted."

I roll over and raise an eyebrow at her. "What?"

"It only works when I want it to."

I throw a pillow at her and she ducks out the door, laughing.

I moan and whine. Then I stretch and follow her to the living room.

Mrs. Snow is already by the door. She smiles at me. "You go on back to bed and get yourself some more sleep, sugar. I don't envy you. That murder business is nasty. You need your wits if you're gonna be hanging around folks like that pixie or Gor."

I yawn as I open the door and hold it open for them. "I will. Sorry I fell asleep."

JR pats my arm. "Don't worry. You'll get to help me tonight."

I'm too tired to even think of a retort. I just lock the door, set an alarm on my phone and collapse back in bed.

I sit straight up in bed, panicked. Then I smack my phone. Stupid werewolf howl alarm. It's the only way to get my sorry butt out of bed at four p.m. I turn the evil thing off and notice a number of text messages from Jacob. He's heard about the murder—Channel Thirteen is airing the story nationwide—and wants a phone call ASAP. Great. My pseudo-dad is worried.

I do the morning ablutions thing and then dial Jacob's number while I make coffee. Shockingly enough, he answers.

"What are you doing up?" I yawn.

"Time change. It's 6:00 here," Jacob answers. "About to climb in a boat to go fishing with the guys."

"Are you wearing a dumb fishing hat?" I picture his salt and pepper hair stuffed under one of those fashion nightmares covered in feathery hooks.

"Fishing hats are not dumb, young lady. And I didn't call to talk about me. How're you?"

"Okay."

"Okay doesn't really mean okay, you know."

"I know."

"Tell me about it."

So, I curl up on the couch with my coffee cup and spill my heart to Jacob. I tell him about meanie-head Flowers. And about the job, as much as I can tell about an open murder investigation.

"You know you need to be careful around Gor, right?"

"The goblin? He just got the Councilor job."

Jacob swears on the other line. "I want you to stay away from him, okay? He's shady."

"What do you mean?"

"Saffron had some cases with him back in the day. Nothing came of it, but I don't trust him."

"Cases? What kind of cases?"

"Some of his associates went missing."

"Were they ever found?"

"Nope."

"Must not have been enough evidence to tie him to it."

"He got off, I know that."

"Well, whoever did this left some physical evidence, so there should be a trail."

"If it starts to lead to him, I want you to turn the other way."

"You do know that I'm working on becoming an investigator, right? I literally am supposed to *follow* the trail."

He growls. "Dammit, Lyon. Just be safe."

"Now you sound like Bennett."

"How's my future son-in-law?"

This prompts a half hour conversation, since Jacob hasn't heard about the breakup. I talk about Bennett's butthead antics. The upcoming study date with Luke. The fact that Bennett wants to accuse Luke of murder at every turn.

"He's jealous, you know. Threatened."

I sigh. "Why can't it just be awesome and amazing to have a love triangle? Like in all the movies?"

"Because you end up hurting someone, sweetheart. And you have a heart of gold. Potty mouth. But a heart of gold."

Tears fill my eyes. "You're biased."

"Hell yeah I am."

"I wish I could hug you."

"Sweetheart …" his voice trails off sadly. "I'm just not ready to go back." I know he's thinking about his estranged wife. How she lied. Cheated.

I feel guilty for letting his mind go there. "I know. Sorry. Technically, though, you're wrong about the potty mouth thing. My mother made sure of that."

"Lyon—"

"Did I tell you I'm learning to curse in Persian? Her little curse master didn't make this sucker foreign language proof!"

He laughs. And I feel like my faux pas for making him remember his ex is forgiven. "Of course you are. So ... do you know who you're gonna choose?"

My chest tightens. "No. What? Why would you ask that?"

"Because the longer you drag this out, the more painful it's gonna be."

"But ... but I've only been on one date with Luke. How am I even supposed to know?"

Jacob chuckles. "You sound panicked. Are you panicked?"

"If there was a paper bag handy, I'm pretty sure I'd be breathing into it, yeah."

"Lyon, I'm clearly not a relationship expert. But I've been thinking a lot. About where things went wrong. When Saffron wanted to run for judge ... I don't think I was supportive enough."

"What?" I sit straight up, spilling coffee on my robe. "No way! We did letters and pamphlets and posters—"

He cuts me off. "I mean my attitude. It wasn't what I wanted. Wasn't the future I saw for us. I wasn't ... her biggest fan."

I go into the kitchen and dab the coffee off my robe. "I don't think that's true."

"It is. I wasn't her cheerleader. I wasn't enthusiastic. I was going through the motions."

I consider that as I grab a bag of jellybeans. This kind of conversation requires lots of sugar. "So, you always have to be like 'rah-rah' for your significant other? That seems unrealistic."

"Don't be a smart aleck. It was her life's dream. She had a shot at it."

"Don't you dare blame yourself!"

"I'm not! I'm just wondering how we got on the wrong path. And anyway, I'm trying to give you the benefit of my life experience."

I speak through a mouthful of jellybeans. "So ... I should have each of the guys try on cheerleader uniforms. That's what you're saying right?"

"I can see you're taking this seriously."

I sigh. Which is hard to do without drooling when your mouth is stuffed full of sugary goo. "I know I need to take this seriously."

"Just keep what I said in mind. Alright? Which of these guys would high five you each night? Who's gonna laugh at your obnoxious and inappropriate sense of humor?"

"Who's gonna be my BFF, right? Got it. Ten four. Roger dodger."

"Lyon," his voice goes down an octave. His serious lecture voice comes out. "It's time ... to catch and release."

I nearly choke laughing. "OMG. Did you just use a fishing term for my love life?"

"Well, if you're allowed to make jokes about it ..."

"Hanging up. Going to work now."

"Peace out home-fry." Jacob signs off and I shake my head fondly as I hang up.

I toss on my workout clothes and grab a suit for later, Jacob's advice still floating through my mind. I really, really don't want to answer his question. I don't know who to choose. I don't know Luke well enough to trust any answer I'd come up with for him. And, in my heart of hearts, I don't know if the answer would be Bennett.

## 13

Seena's over the moon when I get to the Academy. I'm not even through the doors when he whoops and claps me on the back.

"She's responsive!"

Oh shit. I am a bad person. I didn't even go to the hospital to check on Becca. What a jerk. I open my mouth to apologize, but Seena just keeps talking.

"She's not awake yet, but she's breathing on her own and she's responsive to stimuli. They think she'll snap out of it pretty soon. Maybe even tonight. When she does, I'm asking her out for sure."

"I'm so glad she's gonna be okay." I don't know what else to say.

"You'll have to help me think of some way to ask her out. Something cutesy. Girls like cutesy right?"

"Sure." That sounds like the worst idea ever. Worse than JR's wedding sweatshop. Me? Come up with something romantic? Um, my most romantic efforts were all with Bennett. They consisted of a lamb-a-month subscription and an engraved gold watch. Both suggestions were ads in that astrological mag *Cosmos*. (Ads next to articles like the following: 'Make Your Life in the Bedroom Outta This World,' 'Are You and Your Man Star-Crossed,' 'Save Your Love Life from the Black Hole of Boredom.' You know, real literary stuff.) I'm so not creative with the romance thing. I'm edging away when Seena changes the topic back to things I can handle. Like poison.

"Wife's story checks out. Buying a fainting potion from Dove. Bennett's writing her off for now. 'Cause they think the poison is Dormio. Which is a Schedule I potion. Completely illegal. Not the kinda thing a hack like Dove makes. So, on the plus side, I will have a limited number of leads to follow. On the downside, I'll have to be hacking into gang emails and servers."

"Wait. What?"

"I'm gonna have to search that Troll gang the Bloods, the Crypts, even the fairies are rumored to have a drug ring. Of course, they mostly deal in pixie dust. But ... with a Council seat up for grabs—"

I search Seena's eyes. He's totally serious. He thinks the Crypts might be a part of this. Crap. "Have you talked to French yet?"

"Oh yeah, he was at the hospital with me last morning. He was kind of surprised you didn't stop by."

"I passed out." Shit. Shit. Shit. What was that phrase Seena taught me? I mutter under my breath. "Zahré mar!"

"What's that?" Seena asks.

I don't get a chance to answer, because Flowers walks up right then and barks at us to get moving. Torture number one begins. Physical battery. But the entire time, I'm dreading torture number two.

Torture two shows up in a suit as I emerge clean and dressed from the showers around eleven.

Bennett looks hot in his fully tailored blue three piece, but his green eyes are cold. He's a man on a mission. And I know exactly where he's planning to go.

I close my eyes and steel myself for his growly command. It doesn't come. When I peek through my eyelashes, he's right in front of me, bent forward, looking concerned.

"You okay?"

"Yeah, yeah." I try to play off looking like an idiot. (Why does that always happen around him?)

He waits until all the other recruits have filed past, ignoring their stares.

"You know where we're going?"

I sigh. "Yeah."

"Lyon, I'm not doing this to torture you."

I nod, avoiding eye contact. If he didn't want to torture me, he wouldn't make me go. But he's got to prove a point, right?

The car ride is tense. Silence thick as cement.

When he parks, Bennett turns to me. "Just like the other night. You're my shadow. I'll do the talking. No interruptions this time, Ly."

I give a stiff nod and climb out, pulling at the sleeves of my mauve suit nervously. Deep breath.

Luke's office is a clean-cut brick building in the midst of ramshackle warehouses. The windows are the only ones on the block that reflect the moonlight. Every other building is either boarded up or filthy.

Bennett marches in and down the hall like he's been here before. I trail behind, watching a line of workers shape and assemble wheels through viewing windows lining the hall. Ben smacks open the door to Luke's office. I cover my eyes with my hands. I don't want to be here. I don't want to be part of this.

"Hawkins, where were you yesternight?" Ben's voice drops to a menacing growl.

I peek between my fingers.

Luke is standing behind his desk in a crisp collared shirt. He's eyeing me with amusement, completely ignoring Bennett. Next to him is a tatted Hispanic man with thinning hair and slumped shoulders. That guy does seemed cowed by Bennett's vibe. His gaze flickers between Luke and Bennett nervously.

"Mario," Ben narrows his eyes at the new guy. "How's Cookie? She pleased with what happened?"

My eyebrows shoot up. Cookie? Cookie Gonzalez? As in, head of the Crypts?

I eye the tattoos again. Sure enough, it's there. A tombstone surrounded by a circle. On his left bicep. Mario's a Crypt? How well does he know Cookie? What's he doing meeting with Luke? Luke's meeting a member of the Crypts? I'm pretty sure my face turns paper-white. Holy mother eff! Has Bennett been right all along? My eyes plead with Luke. Prove him wrong. Prove him wrong, please.

Luke gives me a soft smile and then turns to Bennett. "Mr. Gomez was just here to pick up an order of shopping cart wheels for Tidbits."

"That money-laundering grocery the Crypts run?"

Mario laughs nervously.

Luke doesn't look the tiniest bit intimidated. "It's a grocery store, yes. In a neighborhood full of trolls. As you can guess, carts don't fare too well out there. They have a standing order to pick up new wheels every six months. If you have a warrant, I'll be happy to show you their purchase orders and the check copies on file for all purchases. Everything is above-board. Just as everything was above-board a week ago with the miniature furniture casters I sent to the brownie commune in Selino. Or a month ago, when you questioned the order I sent out for the W Games. All of those wizards whose custom skateboard wheels were delayed have you to thank."

He lays a flat gaze on Bennett. It's more annoyed than condemning. But I twist to look at Bennett, whose neck is turning red. From embarrassment.

Is Bennett harassing Luke?

"Mr. French. Ms. Fox, if you'll have a seat, I'll get Mr. Gomez's order and be right with you." He sweeps out of the room. Mario shuffles behind him.

Bennett takes a seat with a huff.

Me? I'm just reeling. First, I thought Bennett might be right. All evening, I've been worried about it. Now, I think he might be crazy. Am I that bad a judge of character? Maybe my guy-dar is broken. If that's true, maybe I shouldn't start anything with Luke. How can I trust myself? My thoughts take a downward spiral. I hardly hear Ben when he curses.

"Dammit."

"Huh?"

"Mario looked confused. He's one of Cookie's runners. And he squeals like a pig. If she'd ordered the hit on Bell, he'd probably know by now."

"So … why are we still here?"

"We're here in case Hawkins saw something on his way out the door."

"You don't think he did it?"

"He's slippery. But probably not."

"But yesterday you said he had opportunity."

"Yeah. He did. But what's his motive?"

"So, you dragged me down here, letting me think you're about to accuse Luke of murder when all you want is a flippin' witness statement!"

"Whoa!" Bennett holds up his hands. "I never said that."

I stand. The fact that he didn't, and that I just put *myself* through the shittiest night of worry does not make my anger recede one bit. "Excuse me, sir. I need a moment." I stomp out of the office.

Luke catches me in the hall. "Are you okay?"

"No. I'm an overanalyzing bozo and a doubter."

"Doubter?"

I sigh. "I'm sorry."

He gives a sad half smile. "That doubt have anything to do with me?"

I shrug, not wanting to say it out loud.

He nods. "I get it." He reaches for my hand and interlaces our fingers. "Look. I'm not perfectly clean. I do have that DUI. Partying after the breakup from Georgina. But for the last fifty years I haven't done anything else illegal. Well, if you don't count ..." he trails off and waits until I'm brave enough to make eye contact.

"Count what?"

"Kidnapping."

With that, Luke sweeps me into his arms and sprints down the hall.

I'm not sure if I should giggle or scream. Is he for real?

Luke opens a door and kicks it shut behind us. It's full of boxes piled to the ceiling. Most have labels, so this must be a prep room for shipment. The smell is cardboard and dust, laced with a tinge of oil.

"Greta, can we get a minute?" Luke calls out.

"I'll take lunch," a woman's voice calls back.

"Now that I have you alone ..." Luke raises his hands and wiggles his fingers. He lets his fangs extend. His voice drops. He takes a few exaggerated tiptoe steps toward me. "I vant to suck your blood. Muhahahaha." He throws his head back to laugh. With his fingers still in claw formation he looks like a total doofus.

I stare at him in shock. "When we met I thought you were a hot, bad boy."

He shrugs. "Been there, done that. Have to worry too much about image. And insults. Besides, leather chafes. I'm embracing the silly side of life now."

"Oh?"

"Yes." He tosses an imaginary cape in front of his face and pulls down slowly. He cups a hand to his mouth and whispers, "You're supposed to run away." He winks.

He wants to play a game?

I dash through the maze of boxes at top speed. But no matter which way I turn, Luke's vamp speed is faster. He's always there when I turn a corner. Smiling. Leaning on the boxes. Making silly faces. Jumping out around corners to scare me. Once he appears shirtless, dazing me with his awesome pecs.

"Gah! You're never gonna let me win." I sit on the floor and pout, lower lip out, arms crossed. FYI, suits are not great outfits to pout in. You cannot get maximum arm-crossing grumpiness.

"That's right. Because I'm a winner." Luke zooms up and stops at the last second to sit next to me. He retracts his fangs and reaches for my hand again. "In a better mood?"

I make a face and shrug but I'm fighting a grin.

He helps me to my feet. "I'll win your trust, Lyon. I promise."

My stomach tingles at that. I lean forward—

A throat clears behind us. Bennett's standing at the end of the row of boxes. He does not look amused.

"Fox, you can go to the Baths and start questioning the women there about the wife and her motives."

"By myself, sir?"

Bennett just raises an eyebrow at my question. It's clear he wants to be alone to question Luke.

I toss a worried glance at Luke, who just shakes his blond head and gives me a smile. Okay then, if he's not worried about it …

I stand, walk to the door, and pull it open.

Luke's voice stops me just before I walk out. "See you tonight."

A blast of heat rolls over my back. Oh crap. Bennett's steaming. Literally.

I start to jog down the hall, certain that the building is about to be obliterated. "Remember, dueling in a non-designated area violates statute 38.9!" I shout.

A tiny flame singes my ass.

I double time it out of there.

I'VE NEVER BEEN TO THE BATHS BEFORE. I STARE UP AS MY Broomer zooms off. The big building looks like a block of polished marble from the outside. And then I see why Bennett sent me by myself. A large metal sign outside reads, *'Females Only.'*

Inside, posh does not begin to describe it. If it didn't have women and birds fluttering all over the place, I'd think it was a sculpture museum. There's every kind of birdbath imaginable. Traditional round stone baths. Eight level mosaic fountains with bathing areas on each level. A gigantic pool for the women who want to stay in human form. A giant marble fairy that's swooping, somehow balanced on a wingtip. The left side of the room is covered in mist and I see brightly colored parrots swoop through the haze. I walk toward the other side of the room and see a human statue on a park bench covered in …

I don't think that's part of the sculpture. Sure enough, I stare up and there are golden "power lines" extending over the sculpture. They're crowded with every bright colored species of bird you could imagine. Okay, will be avoiding that side of the room. Gross.

I trot over to the front desk and have to pay a ridiculous entrance fee—thirty-five gold—and then wait because I ask for a receipt. No way am I doing this without getting reimbursed by the office. The hostess sends me off to a locker room, telling me to strip, shower, put my clothes in a locker, and roam around in a towel. I run through all the germ-related lectures JR is gonna give me later for doing this. She brings her own sheets and towels to hotels. Yup. True story.

Still though, the quality of these towels is better than anything I've ever bought for myself. I wonder if the price includes taking the towel home. It should.

As I'm shoving stuff in my locker, I start listening to the ladies twittering around me. Who looks like a good gossip to target for a run-down on Bell's wife?

Luck is on my side this time (after abandoning me earlier during the whole Luke-Bennett debacle). I hear an older woman prattling on about the murder. I wrap my towel around myself, ignoring the twinge where Ben burned me, and head toward the conversation.

"Those poor reporters! Can you believe it? My nephew works over there—doing hair—they sent five out all last night. They had to wait outside the homes of the City Council members. All night. All day. Twenty-four-hour watch. Just waiting to see if that City Council Killer strikes again." The obese woman pats her grey curls and drops a towel. She grabs a shampoo bottle.

"That is so morbid!" replies a woman with green feathers instead of hair. I'm guessing her partial transformation is caused by leaching, not choice, because her feathers are … not the most becoming. Plastered to her head, flat, somewhat dull. I'm guessing duck shifter.

I bat my eyes and approach the pair. "I couldn't help overhearing. I've been so scared since all that aired on TV. I mean, a serial killer, here? In Tres Lunas?" I give a fake little shiver.

Duck woman pats my shoulder, "I'm sure they're exaggerating things. The news likes to sell ads after all."

The naked woman shakes her head fiercely, which shakes other things. "No. From what I hear, Clo has stayed in her home since the incident. She's hired a giant security service. And I mean giant. My nephew sent me a photo. Twenty feet tall." She grabs her phone and swipes to show off a man posted like a tree by the front door of a house.

How do people on the street know this stuff? Does Bennett already know this?

"What about the others?" I ask.

"I know that cat's been about. But you know cats." Both women roll their eyes, like cats are the stupidest creatures in all creation.

Duck Woman cocks her head at me. "You know, I did go by Gor's the other day. He's got a great jewelry collection—"

Naked Lady giggles. "Yes. He's got some pretty sparkles."

They share some inside joke and I try not to shift uncomfortably.

"Never been there," I state.

"Oh, you should, dear. It can be a little intimidating. But thrilling."

"My friend Tabby's been there."

"Oh, you know Tabby Blue?" Naked Lady's eyes gleam. Do I detect a hint of naughtiness? Tabby does have a penchant for gazing at naked shifter men in her crystal ball. And it's unconfirmed, but I'm pretty sure she doesn't mind letting other ladies watch too. I almost caught her and Sarah Snow one time. I think.

"She's such a sweetheart," Naked Lady grins.

Cat shifter a sweetheart? Yeah, they've definitely stared at shifter men with her.

"She's best friends with my neighbor. We've all been working on putting a wedding together."

The fact that I know Tabby makes the two women relax more around me. But I guess Tabby's in their circle of trust. So I'll take it.

"I'm Lyon, by the way," I add.

Naked Lady give me the nod. "Julianne."

Duck Woman smiles. "Matilda."

"Did you know the guy's wife?"

Julianne shrugs. "Seen her around is all."

Matilda taps her on the shoulder, "Isn't she that one with the blue bleed from her beak?" She gestures to her face.

"Yup," I answer.

"Oh, yeah, she's a snot, but there's no bite to her beak. She'll gossip, but if you confront her, she'll totally backtrack. Annoying. Don't know her but have sat at the same table with her. Feathered Fury fundraisers. Heard her talk. Obsessed with travel. One of those birds who never really flew anywhere in her life. You know."

Okay, the wife is pretty much a dead end. But, I'm here and these women seem to enjoy the gossip. Heck, so do I. Perk of the job, I guess. "So … like what else do you know about all these City Councilors? Which one do you think might be next?"

Naked Lady grabs her towel. "Well, if you want my conspiracy theory, I'm not getting in the shower any time soon. Let's head on out to the steam so I can at least get some heat on these old bones."

I follow the pair into the jungle area of the Baths. The area I swore I'd avoid.

The steam is thick and smells of wet feathers. Yuck. My hair's immediately plastered to my head. I can't see more than five feet in front of me. I can't see more than three feet up. That's what really worries me. I wish I had an umbrella.

Julianne and Matilda greet several other women and sit down along a bench in the back where the steam is hottest. Thank goodness they don't shift or ask me to. I would not have an easy time explaining myself.

"Well, I went down to visit Hawk last night—brought coffee —and he was doing Olivia's hair. Seems like they both think that Giancarlo and his assistant were in on it."

I purse my lips. "Why would they think that?"

"Jackie Hanna told them it was his gun. Police haven't released all that yet. But Jackie was on site, can you imagine?"

"Dunno why she hasn't gotten a promotion yet," Duck Woman—I mean Matilda—says. "Her story made national news."

"Oh, there's drama there too. Apparently, that station head is a real sexist jerk off. Hawk says Jackie's rants could be heard all over the station."

"Well, I for one, think that Russo is being framed," Matilda leans forward.

"Why do you think that?"

"There was only one sweet blood nominee. They only had a one in three shot at that Councilor spot. What better way to even the odds?"

I think of Eudora. Military. Strategist. Survived half a millennia. It's not a terrible theory.

"Pixies are notorious for causing chaos. And look at the mess this murder has become," Julianne shakes her head. "She's probably up in her hotel room laughing it up."

"Well, if she gets caught up for that, they'll probably sniff out her pixie dust ring," Matilda makes a disapproving school marm face. "So I hope she didn't do it."

"Wait, what?"

"You think half these chickens would be in the air without her?" Julianne sweeps her hand around the room. "Eudora's the only reason they're all flying."

"I'm lost," I bat my eyes. I really am lost. But I'm trying so hard not to look judgmental and start spouting off statutes right now. Shit!

Matilda leans forward and pats my hand. "You haven't lost that battle with metabolism yet. Once you do, pixie dust is the only way you'll fly. Watch."

She pulls a necklace out of her sagging cleavage, one I hadn't even realized was there. She pops the jewel to the side and takes out a little dust. She sprinkles it on herself and then shifts into a swan. Nobody around gasps, so I guess they're used to this sort of thing at the Baths. She takes flight. Julianne and I watch her disappear into the mist.

"Wow. I feel naive."

Julianne pats me on the hand. "You really haven't ever heard of E? Eudora's been selling dust here for nearly a decade. You better get on her list. Because it's long. And by the time you get to the top of that list, your aching wings will need it."

So, one of the candidates is a dust dealer. Question is, would she kill to hide that secret?

## 14

When I get back to the office, I head straight to Bennett's door. It's locked. I peer through the blinds on his glamorous, hall-facing window. (Perk of being the boss at a government op. The illusion of grandeur.) He's not in there. So I find the second in command on this investigation. Who happens to be my favorite: Diego Flores.

Flower's office is everything you'd expect of a meticulous asshole. Minimalist. Spartan. Box of *Magic Muscle* bars on his desk along with one of those shaker bottles that athletic people use to show off their energy drinks. Whenever I hear those balls clattering in mixer bottles I narrate in my head. Deep steroid man voice: "Yeah, check it out. Stop working and look at me. I'm so hot. You know you wanna be this hot. But you can't. You know why? You can't get over your ridiculous addiction to food. *I'm* not weak like that. I *love* the taste of cardboard." You know what I love to do when I see people drinking those things? Bust out a candy bar. A real one. With caramel. Enjoy it in front of them as they get algae/whey/collagen/pig crap sludge build-up on the roof of their mouth.

Flowers isn't there, but his computer screen is on and a half cup of coffee sits near it. So, I'm guessing he'll be back.

Guess I'll sit and wait. That's when I realize, his office doesn't have chairs. What?

I don't even see one behind his desk. I go around behind it. And of course, there's an exercise ball back there. I'm totally tempted to roll the exercise ball out and start bouncing but Flowers is just a little bit too scary. I mean, you can't be right in the head if you don't even let guests sit in your office, right? Maybe he's such an asshole he never gets guests? I start to think about what kinda guy he actually is. I mean, tiger-shifters are loners by nature ...

Flores walks in before I can dissect his inner workings, looking pissed as usual.

"What do you want, Fox?"

"Sir, I just came from the Baths. I wanted to tell you what I heard."

"You came in here to tell me petty gossip from those feather-headed fools?"

"Nice alliteration." The compliment does not soften his expression. "Captain French asked me to go there and ask around about Bell's wife."

"And?" Diego Flores crosses his ankles and leans against the front of his desk. His eyes dare me to make contact. I'm not brave enough. The man just radiates … fury. "Well, rookie?"

"Some of the women there claim Eudora Daisy's running pixie dust ring."

Silence. And more awkward silence. I risk half a glance at Flower's face. He's stone-cold pissed.

"What was your assignment?"

Is this a trick question? I just told him. "To go ask around at the Baths."

"About whom?"

Crap. "The wife."

"How many people did you speak with about her?"

"Two."

"How many people did you speak with total?"

"Two." My stomach starts to feel queasy.

He closes his eyes and grits his teeth. "Were the Baths empty?"

"No, sir." Yup. Definitely queasy.

"But you choose to talk to two people. Only two."

I bite my lip. Damn Ly. Idiot.

Flores lets me stew in my own stupidity for a minute.

"What did you find out about the wife?"

"She's a gossip. But not good with confrontation. They didn't like her." I'm close to whispering. I'm embarrassed. I can't even believe myself.

"That's it?"

I nod.

"You found out nothing about her relationship with her husband? Nothing that lets us know if she was actually willing to commit murder?" His brown eyes turn into black pits and I'm pretty sure I'm staring at the devil, being judged and found wanting, about to be condemned for all time to a burning pit of humiliation.

"No, sir." I look at the floor.

"So, you found nothing of use to this case whatsoever."

My eyes fly up. "But Eudora Daisy—"

"Lives beyond The Veil, yes? Is outside our jurisdiction ninety-nine percent of the time? Tell me, what kind of proof did the two women you spoke with offer?"

"Umm…"

"Ms. Fox, do you remember our lesson on hearsay? I know it's been a few weeks, and your abysmally tiny brain might find it hard to hold onto information that long, but gossip is not the basis for a case. Shit, I couldn't even get a warrant to search that pixie's tiny, two-inch suitcases based on what you've got."

My face heats. I wish I could disappear. Of course, I can't. Because I have the suckiest powers in the universe. I stare at the floor again. Part of me wishes Flowers would shift, eat me, and put me out of my misery. Because I just discovered I suck. I suck at this job. I made a mistake. I got so gossip-happy that I didn't even stop to think.

Flowers interrupts my pity parade. "Cat got your tongue? Nothing to say for yourself?"

"I'm sorry, sir."

"Sorry for what?"

"Sorry I wasted your time."

"Fox, don't you dare submit that receipt. The department doesn't have the gold to pay for your mistakes."

I close my eyes and nod. Here comes a week of candy corn for dinner.

"To prevent future fuck ups, you're going to get a daily quiz on all the content we've studied so far. After hours, my office."

"Sir?" I'm in a daze.

"You heard me."

"But, when am I going to study?" It comes out aloud, but really, my brain is just reeling. I already have Academy. Then this investigation. Shadowing and writing up the reports for the actual investigators. Then, because I haven't learned to control my powers, I'm usually scrubbing toilets for an hour with whoever else landed on the shit list. Then JR ... how am I going to find time to study, too?

"You're sleeping, aren't you?" Flower's expression is dead serious.

Part of me wants to punch him. But the other part of me sags in defeat. He's right. I can't eff up again.

"Yes, sir. I'll be here."

"And, Fox? Next time you need to sit and think before you run your mouth. Why the hell would a drug dealer kill her customer base? Why would Eudora off a bird if she's wrapped up in dealing to them?"

I open my mouth and close it. I don't have an answer for that. Other than she wouldn't.

I'm a triple idiot.

I turn to leave only to find Seena stepping through the door. He looks almost giddy, in contrast to how I feel. He raises his brow at my expression, but I keep quiet. No way am I admitting how bad I just messed up.

"French wants you both in his office," Seena keeps it clipped and formal, but I can tell he's fighting a grin. He walks a little too fast to be casual when we follow him down the hall. He must have found something. Mother effing dammit! If my mother were more powerful, I'd say she'd orchestrated this whole thing. But unfortunately, fate's just a bitch like my mom.

We crowd into Bennett's office. The ballerina medic from the crime scene—who I officially hate, btw—is standing next to Bennett's chair. Seena scoops his laptop up off the only guest chair in the room and sits, starting to pound away at the keys. So no chivalry there.

Ballerina's talking in her dainty-as-glass, annoying-as-hell voice, "—calculate that the poison was designed to be triple potency. Meaning whoever did it wanted to be sure their target died." Ballerina floats her hands close to Bennett's chest.

I growl internally. Dammit. I have no reason to do that. I just had cutesy moments with Luke earlier. Ignore, Ly-ly. Ignore that. It's over. He didn't fight you. Focus on how you're gonna un-suck at this job.

I search for something else to look at and my eyes land on a bowl of jellybeans on the edge of his desk. Bennett hates jellybeans. The heat of his mouth makes them melt the moment they hit his tongue. He calls them sugar slime. And yet, here he's put out a bowl of them. A tiny smile creeps onto my face.

I glance at Bennett. His gaze is intense. I can't tell for a second if he's still mad at me or not. He basically heard Luke ask me out earlier.

But then he pushes the bowl of jellybeans my way.

Does that mean I'm forgiven? Or that he's accepted our breakup and is moving on?

I'm full of questions as I snag a few beans.

But I'm not getting answers right now. Right now, we're discussing a dead bird.

"Did Bell ghost on you?" Ben turns his attention back to Ballerina. About a third of the time, ghosts of murdered people stick around, determined to catch the killer. Of course, they usually only stick if they don't know who killed them. Curiosity. So, per the Academy slideshow I had to sit through earlier this evening, Bell the Booby sticking around would be a bad thing. I hope Flores' first quiz for me is on ghosts.

Ballerina shakes her head. "Nah, probably glad to escape that wife of his. She's been calling non-stop. When can she pick up the body? Will his body be okay for a sky burial? To which I told her, only if she wants to poison all the birds she feeds with it. Well, that didn't go over well. She about had a conniption. On and on."

Speaking of on and on …

"Okay, well thanks for the update." Bennett's dismissal is terse.

Her response, "Anytime," is laced with innuendo. Totally not classy. Even Seena looks up from his laptop.

Flores interrupts. "Sir, you wanted to see us?"

Thank God he did it. Because I just about destroyed the jellybeans left in my palm.

"Guess that's my cue to leave." Ballerina floats out the door with one last eyelash flutter.

I try not to slam it behind her.

Ben tries to hide his grin, but I can tell he's loving my bitchy mood. Little does he know it's only half caused by stupid girl's flirting. He flashes me a hot look before switching to business mode. So, does that mean he still thinks we're getting back together? He kind of said he didn't mean to break up. What does he want? Gah! I hate non-verbal communication. I suck at it.

"Seena, tell them what you found." Crap. Bennett's sticking to business. Fine. Business. It's what I said I wanted right? It's what I want. Yup. Yeah. Focusing on business.

Seena tries not to preen, but I'm pretty sure his glasses don't need to be adjusted and he doesn't need to sit up straighter in his chair to talk to us. "Clo is pretty careful with her communications. Nothing in her email could suggest too much. But, she did take a potions course at the community college two years ago. And I looked up their syllabus. It includes poisons. Not making them. But discussion. Theory. And ingredients. Dormio's on the list of poisons studied. Clo did her final paper on it. I pulled that up. She noted a couple third world magical leaders love to use Dormio for public executions. Because it appears humane. The victim just falls over. But, it would provide a sound example for the remaining population. Of course, you'd have to widely publicize that it was a murder. She did cite a case in Taklit, Turkey where the population didn't believe a rebel was dead. Months of social media 'sightings' followed."

Bennett stands, "Okay, well I think that's enough detail for now."

We all look to him.

"What are you waiting for? Let's hop in the car and go ask a white witch about her fascination with death potions."

## 15

Clo's not at home. (Home being a conch shell magically enlarged to hold a palatial-sized studio apartment.) The warlock butler tells us Clo is visiting Eudora over at Hearts and Powers B&B. So, we jump back into Bennett's government-issued black SUV and book it to the hotel.

Clo and Eudora are sharing high tea in a doily-infested restaurant to the right of the lobby. We wade through overcrowded, two-chair tables covered in gauzy tablecloths and filled with women wearing over-sized hats. Apparently, tea's a thing. Outside Britain. Who knew? Definitely not me. Some of the teacups hold a red liquid that I suspect is very much not tea. I mean, vamps run the place. I guess it makes sense. Maybe. To someone. Not me. But whatever. Vamp ladies are getting their *class* on or something. I guess neck biting doesn't appeal to everyone.

That makes me wonder how Luke takes his blood. Which is totally off topic. Which makes me bump into Clo's table and spill Eudora's thimble-sized teacup.

"Sorry!"

Eudora just gives me a pitying shake of the head. Clo narrows her eyes. She is makeup free today. And I was right about her scare factor. She looks like an ice carving. Cold, hard in a way that says, 'I'll freeze your blood in your bones.' I'm not sure if she or Gor the Goblin would win a 'my worst nightmare' contest. Maybe her because she's in front of me.

Bennett and Flowers pull another table over and sit. Seena struggles to do the same, so I help him. Underneath all the gauze, the tables are glass. And heavy. Seena and I sit.

Flowers takes the lead, which surprises me.

"Ladies, we just wanted to speak with you a little about the incident a few days ago. We'd like to keep this low-key. With the understanding that we're just looking for more information right now."

"Of course," Clo gives a brief nod, face devoid of emotion. Most white witches are smiley and have a hippy earth-loving vibe. But not her. And I don't know if it's because she specializes in winter spells or because she's secretly a dark heart disguising herself as an undercover spy so she can annihilate the other side.

I have to turn off the conspiracy button in my brain as Clo starts speaking. I'll never beat Seena by coming up with wild and impossible theories. Clues. I need clues.

"We knew, of course, the night prior to the announcement, that Eudora wasn't going to be selected."

I'm the only one who raises my eyebrows.

Eudora sees it and brushes some pixie dust over her throat to speak. "Winner gets notified so they can prepare their speech."

I toss her a nod of thanks.

Clo continues, "Of course, we never planned for Eudora to actually win. The chances of the mayor choosing to upset the balance of representation was very slim."

"May I ask why you nominated her?" Flowers tilts his head as if he's genuinely interested. And I have trouble not staring at him. Who the heck is sitting across from Clo? And where did my hard-ass teacher go? He's gotta be pulling this polite shit out of his ass.

Eudora jumps in. "A Wing position is coming open. Clo's trying to convince me to go for it. She thought I needed a little boost to my resume."

My jaw drops a bit. Wing positions are very rare. Beyond the Veil, they're incredibly powerful. Wings negotiate treaties, work on immigration laws, deal with law enforcement for foreigners. With Clo as a Councilor and Eudora as a Wing, there could be a lot of changes coming for Tres Lunas.

Eudora winks at me. "Yup. Lots riding on that. Wouldn't be a death on the battlefield per se. I'm still not convinced I'm the best fit for the job. I'd still get to carry a sword. But the chattering every day. Not sure how she puts up with all of it. Swords solve problems faster than words."

Clo rolls her light blue eyes at that. "Short term solution."

Eudora turns to her. "Well, now, with a serial killer stalking you all, it does make that sorta job a little more appealing."

This time it's Bennett that interjects. "That's just media speculation."

"I dunno. They're usually right." Eudora gestures to her teacup and Clo somehow manages to refill the tiny cup without spilling any. The pixie takes a sip. "Rumors all start from somewhere."

"Clo, there were some specific items we'd like to ask you about. A few years ago, you took a class at a local community college."

She rolls her eyes. "Which one? Pottery? Magical bindings? Anatomy?"

"You go to community college?" Eudora looks taken aback. "I didn't know that." She almost seems offended. Like she should have been told. Are they that close?

Clo waves her off. "It's just one of those things. The PR rep for the Council suggested we all do more community activities."

Bennett leans forward, trying to keep his voice low. "What we were really interested in was a class you took on potions."

The white witch cocks her head. "Okay. That was a while back."

Bennett gestures to Seena. My Persian pal slides over a printout of Clo's final paper.

Clo's eyes widen as she reads the title. Her pupils dilate. She glances up, and I think I might see worry cracking those ice-like features. "Is Dormio …?" she lets her tone trail off, the perfect politician. Aware that we're surrounded by a group of nosy gossips.

Flowers gives a curt nod.

Clo's eyes widen. She turns to Eudora. "Would you mind if I go to your room for a moment?"

"'Course," Eudora takes a gulp of tea. "I'm gonna flit outside for a smoke." Clearly, the fairy knows something's up.

Clo stands. We all stand. I worry for a second that she's gonna make a run for it. But she scoops up her final paper, threads a hand through Bennett's arm and says, "Follow me."

Looks like she's not gonna run. If she's not gonna run, then she'll probably talk. But whatever she wants to say isn't something she wants overheard.

Seena and I share a glance as we thread back through the teatime mess.

Are we about to get a big break in this case?

As we trot up the stairs, I hear Bennett's radio chirp. He turns off the speaker attached to his shoulder.

Clo unlocks a door on the right and holds it open. We start to file in, but Bennett's cell starts to buzz. He sighs and glances down at it. "Sorry. Have to take this. Go ahead and get started, Flores." He steps back into the hall and lets Flowers shut the door behind him. Of course, he doesn't bother to sit.

The rest of us perch on heart-shaped pink velvet chairs set on a red rug that has little cupids woven throughout.

"Clo, I believe that you wanted to tell us something?" Flowers puts his arms behind his back and waits patiently.

Clo takes a minute to sit and stare at the paper in her hands. "This won't get out right? No reason for it to be in your final reports?"

"I can't guarantee anything until I know what you're going to share."

She sighs. "Of course not. Look, the classes were a PR move, alright? Nothing more. Show up. Mingle. That's it."

Seena stiffens beside me.

"Okay ..." Flowers waits for her to continue.

"Look. My job is stressful. There are a lot of long hours. I don't have time for ... homework. Okay?"

Flowers stays quiet and stares at her. It makes Clo squirm. Heck, it makes me squirm.

Seena clears his throat. "Are you saying your teachers passed you without turning in any homework?"

Clo's cheeks turn the palest shade of pink. "No."

"Are you saying you turned in homework?" Flower's voice is soft, almost gentle.

"Yes."

"And you did not do the homework you turned in?"

She sighs. "Yes."

"Who did it?"

She shrugs. "I dunno. I just went to one of those sites online. Homework Wizards or something."

Flowers tilts his head. "And did you tell them what to write about?"

Clo shakes her head adamantly. "Nope. No time. I'd just scan the assignment pages. Tell them the due date. Pay."

Flowers takes out a notebook and a pen. "Can I get your password and login to the college and to the Wizards site?"

Clo nods and takes the paper from him. "Can this be kept off the record?"

"I honestly can't say just yet. We'll have to look into who was writing those papers for you. Because whoever it was ended up being quite the authority on this poison."

Clo slumps in her chair. "Dammit."

Bennett smacks open the door. "Dammit all." He looks straight at Flowers. "Get what you need?"

Flowers nods and grabs the notebook back from Clo. "Yup."

"Good. Thanks Councilor. Everyone, move out." Bennett stomps down the stairs without another word. And I mean stomps. Even though Hearts and Powers has a plush velvet carpet for the stairs, I can still hear his feet smashing each step.

I give Clo a brief nod of respect and hurry out to the car.

Bennett doesn't speak until he's pulled out of the parking lot and is racing down the street. "I got a call from dispatch. There's a new body."

Well crap on a cracker. Bennett's fury is heating the car. Sweat is pouring down Seena's forehead. I don't speak. I'm not sure what Bennett will do. I'm not sure I've ever seen him this mad.

"Shit. Councilor?" Flowers is the only one brave enough to break the silence.

Bennett shakes his head. "Nope. Looks like the cameraman might have witnessed something that day."

"Cameraman?"

"Channel Thirteen."

My jaw drops. That wimpy weirdo guy? Wizard maybe? Did we even question him thoroughly? I remember he and Jackie were harassing people for interviews.

My gaze flickers sideways toward Seena. Good. At least he looks as floored by this as I am.

My phone buzzes.

*City Council Killer Strikes Again!*

"Um guys? The press knows."

We all have to duck when Bennett's head shifts to dragon and he accidentally spews flame.

## 16

**B**ennett screeches to a halt when we get to the courthouse parking lot. The scent of singed hair is strong in the air, though he managed to get it under control before he burned the leather seats. He's back to full human now and spits out orders. "Flores, you check the tape for anything the camera guy might have caught. Seena, verify Clo's info. Fox, I'll call you with assignments if anything comes up."

Mr. French gives everyone an assignment but me. Favoritism? Or punishment for my date with Luke? He knows how bad I want to prove myself. It's gotta be punishment. I glare at him before climbing out. Fine. Act like you don't need my help. I don't care. You're just the boss. That's all.

I'm about to professionally storm off when Flowers calls my name.

"Fox! You were still on the bottom of the class for spells tonight."

I turn slowly, gritting my teeth. "Yes, sir."

"You get to shred old confidential files. Eight boxes. In my office."

I give a brisk nod, testing my ability to murder him with my eyes. It doesn't work. Disappointing.

"And during that, remedial lecture."

"Looking forward to it." I picture smashing his face with my fist. Whacking him with baseball bat. Throwing darts to watch those stupid perfect muscles pop like balloons. No, I don't hate him. He just inspires violent monologues. That's not hatred, right? That's poetry … with blood.

And hell no. I'm not projecting anything from Bennett. I don't give two shits what that stupid dragon does.

"Yuck fou," I mutter as I trudge behind Flowers down the hallway, unable to end the suckiest day of my career thus far.

Flowers kindly has maintenance drag the boxes and a shredder to his office. But no chair. So, I get to sit on the floor like a two-year-old. Did I say bat? That's too swift. Too good for him. Now I'm thinking rusty nails. Covering his tiger form in duct tape and slowly pulling it off again and again.

Flowers ducks out to check on Seena as I get to work and it's a box of shredding before he rejoins me. The smell of Korean barbecue teases me. Of course, he's going to eat while I work. My violent fantasies take on a cooking edge. Like boiling one toe at a time.

"Tell me what you know about our demographics." He leans against his desk and unwraps some spicy skewers of meat.

"Um ... we're a town of mainly magical creatures?" The shredder gets mad at me for stuffing too many papers down its face. I have to reverse it and rip the papers out of its jaw before starting over. Stupid fricking government. Paying for shredders that only eat five pages at a time.

"Total population?"

"Close to three hundred thousand."

"Two-hundred eighty-thousand give or take. What percentage of the different populations do we have?"

Crap. Numbers. He wants numbers? I rack my brain. I know shifters and fae are a big part of the population. No true majority. I don't think. "Shifters are um... forty percent?"

"Thirty-one point five. How about fae?"

"Um ... less."

Flowers waves a skewer at me. "Less is not a number."

"Twenty …" His head starts to bob and then he realizes he's helping me guess. He stops. No. Don't help me. Of course not. Why help when you can torture? Dickwad.

"Twenty-six-point-three percent."

"Is the point three really important?"

"Yes."

"Why?"

"Because that's what it is."

Oh geez.

"What's the next largest population?"

"Goblins." I'm sure of that only because Becca made a dumb joke about them gobblin' up the competition during class.

"Correct." Flowers gets a call and he takes it out into the hallway before answering.

He shuts me in. And I shred, shred, shred. I take a bathroom break and text JR to let her know I'll be late to wedding sweatshop.

She texts back that they'll set up at Sarah's apartment tonight. I cross my fingers and hope that means the Southern woman will provide a spread. I'm starving. Even Flower's nasty spicy meat sticks are starting to smell appealing.

I get back to shredding and start on a new confidential box. It's about a wife who helped her husband hide his shifter serial eater tendencies. He didn't just like to hunt rabbits. He liked to hunt rabbit shifters. The creep factor is luring me in to flip more pages when my hand starts to itch. Then my fingers swell.

"Shoot! Shot! Shizzle!" I stand. The itch is so bad I can't resist. I have to scratch. But then my left hand starts to itch too. I shake my hands, but the itch is slowly spreading up my arms. "OMG. What's happening?"

"Confidential itch powder. Maintenance must have forgotten to remove it." Flowers leans on the door jamb, nonchalant.

I glare at him. I halfway think he did this on purpose. "You don't happen to have any reversal spells handy?"

"Nope. And looks like everybody's cleared out for the day."

"Of course, they have. Because it's government. Everyone but you has gone home at a reasonable hour. Excuse me." I shoulder past him and march down to the women's restroom. I flip the water on full gush and bend to sink both my arms under the spray. I don't even care that my sleeves get soaked. Thank goodness this itch powder's water soluble and not oil-based. The shit washes right off. Sweet relief. I dry myself with paper towels and exit the bathroom, fully intending to march my ass home and leave Flowers and his stupid shredding behind.

But Flowers has anticipated my anger. He's halfway down the hall, standing with a pair of rubber gloves in his hands.

"We were discussing populations when I left," he tosses the gloves at me. "After goblins, the next largest demographic is vamps. Nymphs, demons, wizards, ghosts and miscellaneous other groups make up the remainder of Tres Lunas." He jerks his head toward his office.

Begrudgingly, I trudge next to him.

"What is the strongest value for shifters?"

"Value?"

"Yes. What do they want to see in pack members, clan members?"

"Compliance?"

"Not quite. Though some twist the value into that. Loyalty. Loyalty is the most important thing for any shifter."

My thoughts immediately stray to Bennett.

"Focus!" Flowers snaps in my face. "Fae. What do they value?"

"Power?" My mother made sure I knew I wasn't valued. No real magic, no real place in society. Or at home.

"No. Cleverness. Fae love to think they're the smartest people in the room. Hence your loud mouth."

"Um … okay. Witches … Clo seems motivated by appearances. With the whole homework thing. And how she somehow thinks getting nominated out here will help Eudora's chances to get a Wing."

"You don't think it will."

I shake my head vehemently. "Fae are snobs. It's not just about cleverness. If they think the human world likes you, they wonder what's wrong."

"Hmmm. Well, maybe that was a lie."

I shrug. "I wouldn't know. But you've got a liar and a professional killer slash part time drug dealer in cahoots on something."

"Did you just say cahoots?"

"I hang out with a lot of old women."

I watch Flowers swallow a smile. "Well, she lied about doing the homework. But Clo didn't lie to us today."

"She paid for homework. Seena verified that?"

Flowers nods.

"So, *he* got to go home?"

Flowers grins. "He wasn't bottom three."

"Hey!"

He ignores my indignation. Because it means nothing to him. His lecture voice turns back on and semi-human, smiling Flowers turns off. "Wealth is what goblins value. Vamps want power. Nymphs love attention. Demons want power via servitude. Wizards vary based on their human motivations. Ghosts want revenge."

"Okay …"

"So … out of our suspects, who'd get their ultimate values fulfilled based on the killings so far?"

"Um …"

"Exactly. Who would want to kill a wannabe Councilor and then a cameraman?"

"Well, I mean, they might only have killed the cameraman to cover their tracks."

"True." Flowers clicks a button on his computer, turns the screen my way, and silent video feed plays. It's from Town Hall. He puts the feed at one and a half times regular speed. We all look like little animated claymation weirdos running around.

"Why aren't we listening?"

"Sometimes you have take away one sense to enhance another."

"You sound like some bad motivational speech."

He's fighting a grin again. Maybe there is a tiny bit of humanity left under all those overblown muscles.

"You know, I don't know if I really believe your value thing. It oversimplifies people."

Flowers shrugs. "Most people are simple."

"My best friend isn't shallow and attention-loving. Captain French rejected his whole family." My heart gives a little twinge as I say that last bit.

"Odd ducks."

I roll my eyes and look back at the video as I feed the shredder. "I think you'd have to have a lot of different emotions surging to motivate you to kill someone."

"Me? No. I just have to be hungry."

I almost lose a finger.

The tiger made a joke.

"You know, it could have been you instead of Becca."

"What?"

"I almost radioed to tell you to go check Mr. Bell's pulse. She'd already done it. Would have given you experience."

My stomach turns cold. I gulp. "It could be me in the hospital right now?"

He nods. We turn back to the video. And suddenly, I'm watching it way more closely.

But even though Flowers and I re-watch the moments leading up to Bernard's death like forty bazillion point three times (I've learned the importance of decimals. Not about to skip out on them during exaggerations anymore), we do not figure out whodunnit.

Mason McDonnelly, the cameraman, seems to have captured days of footage instead of hours. It gets mind-numbingly boring. Until the very end. The video clicks off.

"Wait. That's it?"

Flowers cocks his head. "What do you mean that's it?"

"Where's the feed from the balcony?"

Flowers leans over his desk (standing, of course) and clicks through the different video files. "There is no feed from the balcony."

"But he put a camera on the balcony."

Flowers turns to me as he dials and holds his cell phone up to his ear. His eyes burn into mine.

"Boss? Hey. We mighta' found out why that camera wizard was killed."

## 17

Flowers gets on the phone with Channel Thirteen and confirms they don't have any additional footage. He calls up Seena to try to see if the file was originally downloaded anywhere and if it's 'recoverable' or something. Seena gets to come back to the office. I get dismissed. And it's only three a.m. Woot! I grab a Broomer, preparing to break the news to JR that I have a date in an hour.

A date that, Luke texts, will require a swimsuit.

*What?* This is supposed to be a study date! We haven't progressed to swimsuit level dating yet!

I fret all the way home. Do I have waterproof mascara? I haven't swam since I started the Academy. Will my bikini even fit? I don't know about his biting preferences. I haven't told him about my blood's unfortunate tendency to turn vamps human. Is a bikini too much of a temptation for a vamp? Wait. What about … the tattoo?

JR sees me land and comes outside to greet me.

My anxiety hits her full blast. "Did you tell him about my tattoo?"

"What? Who? No. I haven't told anyone anything."

I grab her shoulders. "Double promise?"

"Yes. Why?"

"I forgot to tell you I have a kinda date with Luke in an hour and he said I need a swimsuit." My eyes are wide with panic. I may or may not be breathing. I'm not sure.

"Whoa Nelly. Calm down, girl." JR pets my hair. "I'll go upstairs, grab you some clothes while you eat. Sarah's desperate to feed you her cornbread fried chicken—"

Food. My mind shifts gears. I moan in anticipation. Sarah drizzles honey over her fried chicken. Yum. Just double yummy fat yum yum.

JR smiles. "There's my girl. We'll play dress up. I'll help find a way to keep your tattoo covered. You can swim with a shirt or something."

"You don't mind that this is interrupting wedding sweatshop?"

She shrugs. "Tabby and Sarah have a handle on it. I got them invited to the wedding. They've really done some amazing stuff. They folded like two hundred cranes tonight while I was at work. And the wings they've been building are gonna be amazing." JR heads toward the stairs.

I head inside, where I'm immediately welcomed, a glass of lemonade is shoved into my hand, and I'm cooed over like I'm the most adorable thing ever. Sarah Snow pours it on.

I really need to move to the South. People in Cali do not greet each other this way. It's like … the difference between cats and dogs. Catitude rules L.A. 'I'm better than you bitches!' Whereas the tail-wagging uber-friendliness of the South is pure puppy dog. I wonder how Snow and Tabby Blue get along if one's like a dog and the other is literally a cat. Opposites? I let my thoughts wander as I eat the most delicious fried chicken in existence, with extra honey.

I eye two mannequins with floor-length feathered wings. "Nice!" I say between bites.

Mrs. Snow smiles at the compliment but keeps working. Tabby's folding paper cranes. She's sprinkling glitter over them. At least, I think it's glitter until some of the bedazzled cranes take flight, flapping around the dining room chandelier like a bunch of moths.

"What is that stuff?"

"Just a little something from a friend," Tabby says as she leans over to turn up the TV.

I stare at the side of her face. She stares determinedly at the television. It's pixie dust. I frickin' know it is. But she won't admit it. Of course not. Is every little old lady into breaking the law? Do they just not care anymore?

I open my mouth but before I get a word out, Jackie Hanna's boobs fill the screen. It's a second before her face comes into focus.

"Tragedy strikes again. The City Council Killer must have more on his mind than just targeting Councilors. He's out to terrorize our community. Show us what a lawless wild west we really live in. What other reason could he have to kill Mason McDonnelly? An innocent who was one of our own. A cameraman I worked with myself on occasion."

"I really don't like her," I sigh. "Why does she get all the coverage?"

Sarah shrugs and sets down a plate of cookies in front of me. "She found the body, I think. Maybe she called dibs."

"That's just gross."

"Real world, honey. Not a pretty sight. Eat up." Sarah grabs my lemonade cup and switches it out for a mug of milk.

"She's not quite as dumb as she seems, you know," Tabby takes a sugar cookie and breaks it in half, watching Jackie go through the timeline of the murders. "I knew her grandma, way back when. Smart nymph. Never got caught with her bloomers down, if you know what I mean."

Sarah's lips thin at that. "Do you have to be so crude, Tabby?"

I crinkle my brow. "What are bloomers?"

"Panties," Tabby smiles at Sarah and eats her cookie. "Jackie's grandma loved the gentlemen. Particularly the married ones. Not so much for commitment. But she never got caught. Not a single wife saw her in action. She was pretty handy with her spells."

Sarah rolls her eyes as she finally finishes her hostess duties and sits back down with us. "Doesn't mean she was a genius."

Tabby pushes her glasses up her nose and her tongue snakes out to grab a lingering crumb on her chin. "She might not have been magenta, but she wasn't the dullest crayon in the box either, Sarah."

Sarah sighs. "Well, there's no telling if any of those brains passed down to her granddaughter."

"Her rack certainly did," Tabby snickers as she turns back to the TV. She ignores the crumpled napkin Sarah tosses at her.

Jackie's showing off said rack as she leans toward the camera. "Channel Thirteen has an exclusive interview with Mason's mother regarding this tragic incident."

The screen cuts to Jackie and an elderly woman sitting on a cramped futon. A poster of a rainbow with some fluffy clouds hides half of the wood-paneled wall behind them.

"Tell me, Ms. McDonnelly what was Mason like?"

"He was a good boy. A shy boy. Loved to read. Tinker. Study. I mean, you knew him Jackie. Wouldn't hurt a fly."

Jackie nods and pouts her lips in sympathy. "He still lived here at home, right?"

I grab one of Sarah's lemon cookies and take a bite.

"This was his garage apartment. He was saving up for his own place," his mother sits up a little straighter, pulling at her button-up sweater. "I think … he might have met someone."

"Ooh! Did Mason have a boyfriend?" Jackie leans forward, tragedy set aside for juicy gossip.

"Boyfriend? No. He wasn't … I don't think he was gay." His mother glances up at the rainbow poster and sighs. "I guess … I guess I just don't know. Now, I'll never know." She tears up.

"Do you know anyone who would want to hurt your son?" Jackie uses her manicured claws to pat Mason's mother on the shoulder.

"No. I mean, not for personal reasons. But I do know one man ruthless enough to do something like that."

"Who?"

"He's a cheater and liar. And a thief. Of course, I guess that's why he got elected right?" the woman's eyes fill with tears. "Gor the Goblin is a dark-hearted monster. And there's no doubt in my mind he's the City Council Killer. He cut down his competition for Councilor. And then, because my son saw something, he killed my son. A boy he'd known—just killed him." She dissolves into sobs.

I inhale. Has Bennett seen this? Is Flowers watching? This woman just accused our new City Councilor of a double homicide. On TV. Also, why the heck are they inside a dead guy's apartment? Shouldn't that be sealed off? What could Mason have seen? I reach for my phone, my mind on overdrive.

The phone is plucked out of my hands. JR dangles it between her fingers.

"Uh-uh. No way. No murdiferous thoughts right now."

"But, this is a big deal."

"Nope. We only have forty minutes to get you looking like a sexy schoolgirl for study time."

"But Bennett—"

"Is a big boy and can handle this without you for two hours."

I turn pleading eyes to Tabby and Sarah.

Tabby shrugs. "I've told you to go for Bennett, but I've been outvoted. At least temporarily."

JR glares at her for speaking out of turn. Then she reaches down and swivels my chair away from the TV. "Sit still. I'm about to do some magic ... with makeup."

## 18

I meet Luke at the Ventura pier. I glance self-consciously around as my Broomer zooms off into the sky, but at four a.m. only bums and jacked up college kids are out. None are close enough to make out facial features. We should be okay in this human town. I hope.

Luke holds out his elbow to escort me down to the beach. He has a picnic basket and a blanket over his arm. His blond hair glimmers in the moonlight.

"Picnic on the beach? I thought we were practicing losing things."

"We are." He grins and leads me toward the water. The wind off the ocean has an extra bite. I shiver as he spreads out the blanket. I can almost taste the salt on the air.

"Why here?"

"Full of questions tonight, aren't you? Did you wear a suit, like I texted?" He grabs the back of his shirt and hauls it off, leaving me gaping at abs that could only be supernatural.

Half-clothed, my Viking fantasies about him seem even more real. I completely forget all questions as I spot the line of hair extending from his naval to his board shorts. OM double G.

"My eyes are up here."

I squish my eyes closed. Humiliated? Oh yeah. But my lady parts are cheering, roaring, doing back flips.

"I showed you mine. Your turn."

I peek. His blue eyes sparkle expectantly. Almost hungrily. And part of me really wants to toss off my cover up dress right there. But … "Um … there's something I need to tell you."

Luke pauses. I think he can hear the tremble in my voice. He steps closer. "Yeah?"

"Yeah." I step out of my flip-flops and wiggle my toes into the sand. Damn. I do not want to say this. Should I just wear the ugly cover up t-shirt JR found?

"So, if we're gonna go swimming … Wait, do we have to swim?"

"We definitely do now."

"Why?"

"Well, whatever you're nervous about is frickin' adorable."

"But … I really need practice."

"It's part of the plan for practice."

"Yeah?"

"Yup."

I sigh. My brain says, *He's not wearing a t-shirt. You shouldn't wear a t-shirt. Just tell him.* "Okay, but before I take off the dress …" I bite my lip. "This is embarrassing."

Luke chucks me on the shoulder. "More embarrassing than admitting to a food fetish on a first date?"

I laugh. "Maybe? But JR's been holding it over my head. Threatening to tell coworkers, you—"

"Just rip off the band-aid."

"When I was nineteen, I got a tattoo."

His eyes start to glitter with amusement. "It's not a fairy on your lower back is it?"

I chuckle. "Nope. Missed that bandwagon. Um … it was supposed to say, 'Candy girl.' Because of my sweet-tooth. But the guy used a naughty needle."

Luke bursts into full on laughter. "Yes!" He punches the air. "Why wasn't this your fun fact on our date?"

ANNA DARE

"It's embarrassing!"

"I want to see it."

I look around. The beach is empty. "Um. This is still public. It's on my inner thigh."

Luke takes a step toward me. "Even better."

"But—"

He leans in. His breath brushes my ear. "Lyon, you take that dress off now or I will help you take it off."

His words send erotic chills down my spine.

"I thought you said you gave up the bad boy thing."

"If the situation calls for it, I'm happy to take control." He demonstrates by yanking me against him. I feel his washboard abs pressing against me. His strong hands grab both of mine and pin them behind me. He uses one hand to keep my wrists in place and the other to slide my sweater off my back. I'm left with just my sun dress. He releases my hands. "Your turn. Show me."

"Okay." I take a step back and meet his eyes. I slowly push the straps of my sun dress down my shoulders. My breathing hitches. So does his. I push further, letting the top pool around my waist. Luke's hands cover mine and together we slide the dress down my hips until it falls at my feet. I'm left in my yellow bikini.

His eyes are dilated. His breathing is ragged. "Now sit. And spread your legs."

I feel naughty. But I kind of like it. So I do.

Luke crouches down between my legs. He runs his hands from my knees toward my thighs, pulling them even farther apart.

My heart races. This should not be happening in public. Part of me wants to check and see if anyone else is watching. But I can't pull my eyes away from Luke.

His gaze falls on my tattoo. And then he bursts into raucous, sexy-mood-ruining laughter.

I cover my eyes. I can't look.

"What's it say?"

"Bite my cookie, Sugar," Luke pants out the words between laughs.

I breathe a sigh of relief. "Oh. That's not as bad as most days."

"Give it a sec. It's rearranging itself."

I glance down as the ink swivels around my inner thigh, forming new letters. Now it says, "Hey sucker, gonna suck her?"

Luke's laughter must encourage the enchanted tattoo, because a second later, more new words are forming.

"Get your Honey Bites here!"

"Bet you're a jawbreaker."

And then, "Watch out for fudge!"

Luke falls into the sand, grabbing his ribs. "I can't watch anymore. It's hilarious."

"Yes, that's what every woman loves to hear when you're staring at her girly bits. It's a total mood-killer. That's why I had to show you now …"

He sits up and cups my cheek, getting sand all over me. "It's perfect. It's totally you." His hand runs a soft trail over my neck. Up and down.

He's forgiven as my libido takes over and wipes all insulted embarassedness from my brain. He puts his body right next to mine. An inch away. Almost touching skin to skin. But the only place he touches is my neck. His fingers glide up and down.

"Swim with me?" he whispers.

"Sure."

He gets up and grabs something out of the picnic basket.

"What's that?"

"This is for your lesson." He nods toward the water and we walk down together, not touching. But my neck is still pulsing from his fingers. I bet he can hear it.

We get our feet wet and my toes curl. "It feels like I'm dipping my foot in ice."

"Good." Luke pulls me into his chest and cradles me there as he wades waist deep into the water. He's not warm, but the way he makes my blood rush does the trick. Our eyes meet, and flirt, and say all kinds of things we don't say out loud. Luke leans down. I think he's going to kiss me. My heart flutters.

His lips brush my ear. "Take these. And back up."

He drops a crinkled plastic sheet into my hand. I look down, trying to hide my disappointment at the aborted kiss. In my hand are a dozen little red and pink heart stickers. Like the kind a second-grade girl hordes in her pencil case. What? I glance up, confused.

He smiles. "Back up a couple feet. Then I'll explain."

I wriggle out of his arms and back up. I regret it for two reasons. One, it's freaking cold! And two, I kinda miss his arms.

"Okay, so, now what?"

Luke ducks his head and bites his lip. Almost like he's embarrassed. "Now, I want you to lose your heart … s." He tacks on the 's' at the last minute. "To me."

Pinch me. I'm in shock. I mean, is this guy for real? I have to hold myself back from launching right at him. What the mother eff? Is that not the cutest, cheesiest, sweetest? My mind reels.

My body brings me back to reality. I'm trembling with the cold.

"O-k-a-ay," my teeth chatter. I peel off a sticker.

"I've lost my heart to Luke." The sticker disappears. But it doesn't reappear in his hands.

"Maybe be more specific?" he suggests. "There are a lotta Lukes out there."

I peel off another. "Do we have to do this in the water?" My hands shake from the cold. It's seeping into my bones.

"It's motivation and a distraction at the same time. Ignore the cold. Try to focus. The sooner you get it, the sooner you get out."

I try to ignore the water. The seaweed tangling on my calves. I stare at Luke, and then the little heart sticker on my fingertip. "I've lost my heart to Luke Hawkins."

Again, the sticker just disappears.

"Dang it!" I pull off a third. I'm frustrated. And worried. I need to learn this stupid shit so Flowers will get off my case. I also want to get out of this water. I want to snuggle Luke. I want to run my hand over those washboard abs.

"I've lost my heart to Luke Hawkin's abs." Whoops. My cheeks flame. That just sorta slipped out.

Luke laughs as the sticker disappears. Then he gives a giant yell, punches the air, and splashes me.

"Ahhhh!! Why did you do that?"

He jump-walks through the water to stand right in front of me. "Look!" He points at his six-pack and I see a tiny red heart sticker.

"I did it!"

"You did it!" He sweeps me up into a bear hug and swings me around.

"Can we get out of the water now?"

"Prove it wasn't a fluke first." Luke sets me down and backs up. He makes me 'prove it' twelve more times. Twelve successful times. Thirty tries total. My fingers are numb. My right leg burns. I don't think I have toes anymore. And I learn that frustration and annoyance greatly help improve my powers. Fricking great. As if they weren't lame enough. I need to be somewhat annoyed or freaked or something to use them.

Once Luke's satisfied, he sweeps me into his arms and rescues me from the subzero sea. He gently sets me on the picnic blanket. He reaches into the basket and grabs a palm-sized purple envelope. A special-order spell package.

"What's that?" I peek.

He opens it, and immediately we're enveloped in heat and light. It spreads like a bubble over us. Like we're out tanning mid-day in the summer. It leeches into my bones and chases the cold away.

"Is that safe for you?"

"Yup. Not real sun."

"Won't people notice?" I ask out of necessity, but I'm already arching my back like a cat.

"It's shielded, don't worry," Luke lays back on the blanket. His torso is dotted with little hearts. The sight makes me smile.

I lean back on my elbows beside him, enjoying the heat, the relaxation. The company. "Thanks," my voice comes out shy and breathy.

"No. Thank you. For giving me your heart." Luke turns his face to mine with a little smile, half-joking, half-not.

Our eyes lock. And my stomach drops. My mouth dries out. I lick my lips and his eyes follow the movement. I want him. But I'm scared. I mean, what he just said ... that's scary right? Because, like, we barely know each other. And there are way more things he needs to know about me. And, and—

He leans toward me. I lean toward him.

And my mouth blows it. "You know, you had a chance to pick panty stickers or something. Then you would have heard me say I lost my panties to you a zillion times."

He laughs and I feel it on my neck. I want to feel more.

"Nah," he breathes. "Then you wouldn't be able to tell Mrs. Snow all about today."

I raise an eyebrow. "So, the hearts were for her benefit?"

"Nope." His lips feather over my jaw. So close to my lips. Closer. Closer. He stops at the corner of my mouth. "They say if you repeat something often enough, you start to believe it."

He doesn't kiss me. He leaves me, panting, breathless, and lays back down.

Swoon.

If I didn't lose my heart to Luke just now, I've come very, very close.

## 19

I have trouble sleeping. I just keep reliving that study date with Luke. When my alarm goes off early at three p.m., I'm already awake. I sit up, energized. Excited for the night.

I get to the Academy an hour early and head straight to Flower's office.

I picture his annoying face and say, "I lost my yoga block in Flower's office." A block zooms over my head to land right on his desk.

Bam Mutha Fucka!

Once every yoga block in the building is in there, I start adding yoga balls, training mats, kickboxing dummies.

My right leg burns as I lose the third dummy. I must have done something to hurt it last night. I shake it out and move another. Ignore the pain, Ly. Focus. Like Luke taught me.

I can't freaking wait to see the look on Flower's face. I've almost got the room full when I hear a noise behind me.

I whirl around.

"So, you figured it out." Flowers casually sips his coffee.

"What? That's it? That's all you have to say? Look at that!" I gesture behind me and turn to look at the lopsided pile. "Look at my magnificence!"

"You need to have that cleaned out before class starts." He turns away without batting an eye, without a shrug, without … anything.

It's so deflating.

I hate him. I start 'losing' things back to their original positions, hoping one or two 'accidentally' hit him on their trip home.

Of course, I'm not that lucky.

Flowers comes in when I'm nearly done. He dials a number and puts it on speaker phone. I turn to leave but Flowers waves at me to stay.

"Flores, what's up?" Bennett's driving in. I can hear his blinker.

"McDonnelly's autopsy is in."

"Already?"

"Shot."

"With Dormio?"

"Nope. Just a regular nine-millimeter."

"Hmm …"

"Yeah, that's what I thought."

"Sorry," I interject. "There must be some kind of secret pro-investigator undertone to this convo that I'm missing."

"Morning, Fox," Bennett greets me.

"The M.O." Flowers leans against his desk.

Ben expands, "Why have such a complicated murder on the front end and then switch to regular old bullets?"

I get my geek face on. "Maybe intended victim matters? A shifter versus a human? One's harder to kill."

"Maybe, but the first indicates a stronger affinity for potion-making. The lab said the Dormio was mixed strong, and Seena hasn't found a trail back to any known gang members yet. So, chances are it was a homemade batch." Flowers rips open a Magic Muscle bar and takes a bite. He doesn't offer any to me. Not that I'd want that nasty thing, but … how rude!

"Where was the cameraman found?" I'm behind. I missed half the newscast between stuffing my face and getting it painted.

"Body was found in a park near his office. Jackie Hanna found him," Ben replies.

"And what the heck was she doing at the park?"

"Said she was meeting the owner there to 'chat.'" Flowers uses air quotes.

"Oh yeah?"

Flowers shrugs. "He confirmed it. Said they were meeting about a promotion."

"She's so trashy."

"She's a reporter," Ben says. As if the two words go hand-in-hand.

"So, what now? Two murders. Two different guns. Are we looking at a serial killer who's trying to throw us off the scent? Or two killers?"

"Two killers?"

"Two killers?" Flowers repeats Ben's question. He cocks his head and stares at me. "Fox, you might have a brain in there after all."

Is it weird that I take that as a compliment?

Seena walks in just as I'm about to tell Flowers how amazing said brain is.

"Becca's awake and talking!"

Shit. My guilt meter goes off. I really *have* to go to the hospital at the end of the night.

"She have any ideas on the case?" Of course, Flowers doesn't ask how she's feeling. That would be irrelevant.

"No, but I did scan McDonnelly's laptop. Looked like someone cleaned it out pretty good. Deleted a lot of files permanently. But they weren't thorough enough." Seena does that push-the-glasses-up-the-nose thing. I think it's his tell for 'I have big news.' Damn. I do not want him raining on my parade when I just got a backhanded compliment. Stupid pony.

"Mason had an underground business a couple of years back. Guess what it was?"

"Stripping!" I squeal.

Seena rolls his eyes, "He wrote exam papers for college students. Couple hundred gold a pop. Guess which City Councilor used his services?"

"So we have our Dormio expert," Bennett's voice is garbled by static. "—Just a minute—parking—right there."

I'm blown away. "So McDonnelly wasn't just some witness. He was a killer." That nerdy guy holding the camera? I barely gave him a second glance.

"Whoa! We need a lot more proof than a paper he wrote years ago," Flowers scoffs.

"There was no footage from that camera on the balcony."

Seena jumps on board with me. "He could have used that camera as an excuse to sneak the gun up there."

I snap my fingers. "Yes!"

"Still speculation," Flowers hedges.

"His mom hates Gor. Accused him on TV of killing her son."

Flowers pinches the bridge of his nose. "Didn't we talk about hearsay, Fox?"

I ignore him. I have a feeling I'm on the right track.

"What if ... Bell wasn't the target? He was standing right next to Gor. Stepped up and shook his hand. What if McDonnelly tried to kill Gor and missed?"

Bennett walks in the room. "If he did that and Gor found out, he'd be a dead man."

"Exactly!"

Flowers rolls his eyes.

I hold up my hands, "We should go question Gor. That's all I'm saying."

Bennett jerks his chin at Flowers. "Get someone to cover Academy exercises this evening. If Gor gets squirrelly, we'll bring him in for further questioning."

Flowers clenches his jaw but starts texting.

"Um, sir?" I'm hesitant. I really want to go, but I don't know where I stand with Bennett right now. "Should Seena and I …?"

"Go get in the car before the other recruits see."

I try not to skip down the hall.

As Seena and I pile into the backseat like eager five-year-olds about to go for ice cream, he leans over and says, "I made the connection between McDonnelly and Dormio. I found the killer. I win."

"Yeah, well, your killer might have killed the wrong person. And my killer might have killed your killer. So, who found the better killer?"

"You haven't proven your killer."

"Yet. If I do, it's a draw."

Seena turns to face forward. His face is way too smug. "Good luck, Loser."

I'm gonna prove this case so hard he's gonna feel it like a punch to the face.

Gor's Pawnshop is stuffed into a strip mall. A sign that looks like it got dragged back from Vegas uses a couple classy neon arrows to alert customers it's here. If that weren't enough, the 'Face You Can Trust' billboards are behind the shop. In case you get confused. Which trolls can do. So I guess it makes sense.

Inside the store is crowded. Not with people. With stacks of crap. There's hardly enough room for us to walk single file through the twisted aisles.

"Spread out. Find him. Let him know we need to verify a few things from his witness statement. Nobody start questioning 'til I'm there," Bennett states.

I don't know why he looks at me when he says this. I don't want to question a killer alone!

We all go different directions.

I go past a glass jewelry display case that's spinning on its own. Necklaces hang suspended in the air around naked lightbulbs. They look like tacky chandeliers. A locket zooms down to hover in front of me and doesn't fly off until I bat it away. Then a pair of flapping poison rings do the same. Talk about pushy sales tactics. Why did those bird-women rave about this place?

I head over to the used book section. The spell books are all chained to the shelves, so at least they won't try to take my eye out.

I see a hooked nose just around the corner of a bookshelf. I hurry forward, but someone barrels into me from the side. Seena beats me to Gor.

"Tres Lunas Investigation," he flashes his ID. "Sir, we'd like to follow up with you about a few statements you made."

Gor doesn't respond. Doesn't blink. He looks … blank.

"Sir?" Seena tries again.

I watch for a few seconds. Gor doesn't move. Doesn't breathe. I reach forward and gently push on him with my finger. He bobs backward and snaps back up, wobbling.

"Zahré mar!" Seena's jaw drops.

"I've heard about these. Balloon dummies of yourself. Didn't know they looked so life-like." I circle the fake Gor. Damn. No wonder Tabby used these decoys in class. It looks real. I push it again, just to watch it bob.

"Stop that! It's creepy."

"I want one."

"Why?"

"I dunno. Freak out the neighbors. Scare school children. Who cares? The spell work is amazing."

"So … why would he have decoys in his shop?"

"Maybe he's made a break for it," I pitch my tone breathy and dramatic.

I hear a throat clear behind me. I whirl around. And Gor the goblin is standing right in front of me. My heart stops.

"Give you a discount if you buy one and use it on school children. So long as I get a video," his beady eyes gleam. My pulse races. "I didn't make a break for it. But I'm guessing you lazy badges finally caught up."

"Caught up with what?" I can't resist asking even as Seena radios Bennett and Flowers. Damn. Lyon. Control your mouth. No questions.

"That whoever did this might have been after me. That they still might be after me." Gor nods toward the rocking dummy. "I have three of those set up in here. With a serial killer on the loose, can't be too careful." His tone is way too light for me to believe he's actually scared.

Me, on the other hand? Currently trying to hide my quaking knees.

"Councilor," Bennett reaches us. "We'd like to talk to you further about the Bell case."

Gor nods, hooked nose nearly touching his neck. "Follow me to my office."

He leads us through the maze of the store. Past racks of half-invisible clothing that look like they've seen better days. Past a set of swords that swing dangerously close to our heads. He puts his hand on the only blank stretch of wall in the entire store. It slides open, revealing a hidden office behind it, complete with a crackling fireplace and red carpet. I feel like I'm walking into the devil's lair.

I exchange looks with Bennett and he positions himself between me and Gor. So his chivalry's not dead at least.

The door seals us in. I clench my hands and teeth, trying to hold back a scream. What the hell? I glance at Seena. He hasn't wet himself, but he looks at least as terrified as I feel.

"Sir, I'm going to spray a horror neutralizer. Looks like my newbies aren't quite used to your ... magnetic personality." Bennett reaches for a canister on his hip. It looks like pepper spray, or striped polecat spray (strong enough to stop three lion shifters in their tracks). He unleashes the spray over us and I squeeze my eyes shut. It smells ... like old lady perfume. Powder and potpourri. At least it doesn't stink.

Seena snorts next to me. Well, maybe not so pleasant for horse noses.

But we can breathe again. The suffocating terror is gone.

"Good?"

We nod at Bennett and he turns back to Gor. "Sir, can you think of anyone who'd want to kill you?"

"I'll print you the list." Gor turns to a computer that looks like it might be an original Apple. Tan box. Black screen. Green letters.

Seena's eyes bulge worse than they did a moment ago. "You don't seriously use ... *that?*"

Gor chuckles. "I specialize in unique objects. And discretion. Not technology."

Seena bites his lip and I can tell he's holding back.

Gor's machine hums like an insect. We wait.

My eyes naturally slide to Bennett and I find him looking at me. I give him a small smile. We're here, following my gut, but I'm not sure where to go next. How can I prove Gor killed that guy? I don't want to let him down.

"Oh, I have to load more paper. One second," Gor goes to a box in the corner and pulls out dot matrix paper (that kind from the nineties that's edged in holes). He feeds it into the printer. And one page slowly eeks out.

"Excuse me," Seena bolts from the office. I don't think he could bear another second of techno-torture.

I step closer to Bennett. "Can I ask a question or two?" I whisper.

He gives a tiny nod.

"Sir?" My voice is a little squeaky. "How did you know Mason McDonelly and his mother?"

"I dated her for four years. Too bad about her son. Though I have to say, he's in a more peaceful place now."

"I'm sorry, what?"

"When you look like I do, you make some allowances when you date. But Patricia, she can nag like no other. Borderline harassment. Since I broke off our engagement, she's been here five times, going on about this and that."

I nod. Trying to look sympathetic when all I can think is— she said yes? WHAT? But that is not what I should be thinking.

"What kind of things was she mad about?"

"Thought I took the toaster oven. Then her engagement ring. Then just to be mad, I guess."

"What about her son? Did you two get along?"

"He was a closed off, shifty kid. Don't blame him with his mom. Hid that girl he was dating. Hid the projects he tinkered with. Kinda just sat there with his TV tray like a lump on a log."

If Mason's mom is really such a nag, gets her heart broken, and suddenly all her attention is focused on nitpicking her son … I can see Mason getting ticked enough to want to kill Gor. Maybe.

But I'm really not getting a guilty vibe from Gor. Not an angry at Mason McDonnelly vibe. Or even a 'I did it and hid it' vibe. Dang.

If I'm wrong and Gor didn't kill Mason, who the heck did?

## 20

I ask if I can step outside for a second. Bennett nods.

I head into the parking lot, trying to piece the bits of evidence together. I led us in the wrong direction. Flowers is right. I need to look at the evidence. I stare at the sky, my mind as blank and empty as it is.

My phone buzzes in my pocket. I pull it out. It's JR.

"I've lost the ring!" she whisper-yells through the phone. Her voice sounds like one of those crazy people who talk to themselves.

"Ring?"

"Shh! I don't want her to hear. The wedding ring! Dress rehearsal. Remember? It was in my hand. Then Camilla needed help with her dress for the bathroom. I was lifting it up. All five hundred pounds. Now it's gone."

"Wait. She was in her dress for rehearsal?"

"The idiot nymph takes dress rehearsal literally. Plus, she'd use any excuse to get photos of herself. But focus. The ring!"

"Well it's got to be in the bathroom."

"No, I thought it was in the chapel. Duh! Not stupid enough to call you before I searched the bathroom. On my hands and knees. In my dress."

"You're never touching me again. Hepatitis. Hepatitis."

"Not helping, Ly-ly."

"Where's Danny?"

"I can't have him come into the women's restroom!"

I bite my lip. "Well … what about her dress? Does it have lace? Could it have gotten caught?"

There's a long pause on the other side. Then a sigh. "She's gonna freak out."

"Who says you have to tell her? Just say you think you see some specks of dirt on the dress and you want to get them off. Or that some of her bodice jewels look loose. Make something up."

"That will still make her freak out."

"Yeah, but bridezilla will be freaking out about the dressmaker not you. Lesser of two evils." I shrug.

"Ugh. I wish you were here."

"Pretty glad I'm not."

"Witch."

"Nope. Fairy." I can picture her unwilling smile on the other side of the line.

"The ring, Ly-ly. I lost the ring!"

"You'll find it. I believe in you."

All I hear is a sigh. Then a dial tone.

At least I've helped someone solve something. The case is another story. I turn back to the pawnshop and stare at it.

The ring. For some reason, that word floats around in my head. The ring. Gor gave one to McDonnelly's mom. She accused Gor of taking it back. An engagement ring ...

"Was that call related to a case?" Bennett's tone is pure boss-ass. I hate it. Hate the tension between us.

He and Flowers come out of the shadows in front of Gor's like two creepy crapheads.

"Umm... the case of the missing wedding ring!" I'm fumbling for words, just anything to get his glare to stop. But then somehow, that phrase clicks. The missing wedding ring.

I pull up the footage from the mayor's Councilor announcement.

"Get closer. Watch," I order Flowers and Bennett to crowd me and stare down at my phone. Seena rounds the corner and joins our huddle.

Jackie Hanna comes into the frame.

"Look!" I point at her.

The men look at me like I'm some ridiculous contestant on some game show. Not like I'm a freaking genius. I point and speak like a preschool teacher. "This is Jackie Hanna. She is interviewing the candidates before the mayor's announcement. Notice anything?"

They stare back blankly.

"The hands boys. Look at the hands."

They squint up at the screen. "She has nail polish?" Flowers —for the first and probably only time in his life—sounds tentative.

I groan. "She's wearing a ring! A ring with a big emerald. An engagement ring."

They look at each other. Then back at me.

"She is *not* wearing a ring later."

I fast-forward to Bernard's second collapse. Jackie's gesturing at the camera, an extra button in her top suddenly undone. I turn to the guys. Their focus is clearly not on her hands. Where it should be.

I clear my throat. "Ahem. See? Ring gone."

"So?" Flowers raises his brow.

Don't trust me, Muscles? It's on.

I march back into the shop and bang on the hidden door to Gor's office. It slides open. This time I don't even blink at the 'eau de horror.' I have more important things to do.

I hold up the video and hit replay. "Sorry. One last question. See this ring? Is that the engagement ring you gave McDonnelly?" I ask as I hear the guys come up behind me.

Gor peers at the screen. "Yes. Why does that trashy reporter have it?"

"What kind of ring was it?"

"1932 emerald poison ring with a twenty-four-karat band."

"A poison ring?" That throws me for a loop. Though it fits.

I hear Seena give a little snort behind me. He knows I'm right this time.

"You said Mason had a girlfriend?" I verify with Gor.

"Yes. Saw a woman sneaking out at noon a few times."

"Jackie interviewed his mother. She deliberately asked if he had a boyfriend. If they worked together, she'd know he had a girlfriend, right? Why would she do that?" I turn to look at Bennett.

That hot, intense stare is back. Yes, Mr. French. I'm on the right track. I know it. You know it.

I continue, "She'd only do that if she were trying to cover her tracks. If she and Mason teamed up for the first murder. If they were together. If Mason stole that ring and gave it to her. If she helped her boyfriend go after the goblin that ruined his life."

"Speculation," Flowers retorts.

"Where'd the ring go? How do you lose a ring in an hour? If you're in a massive wedding dress that's being held overhead as you cop a squat, sure, a ring can get dropped. Get lost in a sea of ruffles. Snag on a bed of lace. But one on your finger? Uh-uh."

"Mason mixed the poison. She smuggled it in," Seena breathed.

Gor sits down in his desk and strokes his chin. "Maybe. Maybe."

"It would be pretty easy to sneak poison past the cops at the door doing magic checks by flashing her cleavage. Cause those things are eye magnets for boys."

"Say your theory is true, how'd they get the gun?"

I turn to Flowers. "You did notice her going off with Russo when we had a break, right?"

He shrugs. "So?"

"So, I bet they got nice and cozy during their off-screen time. Jackie seems to use her nymph talents to her advantage. Wouldn't have been hard to snag that key he keeps in his pocket. Remember how he couldn't find it right away?"

"Her boyfriend would let her do that?"

Gor tosses out. "He's a pushover. And, that family doesn't let go of a grudge. That's for sure. It's possible. If she told him it was the only way."

Seena jumps on my bandwagon again. Guess solving the crime is more important than competing at this point. "Jackie could've handed off the key and the ring to McDonnelly, he could've planted the gun and camera at the same time, then she smuggles the key back. Remote spell detonator would have been easy to keep in his pocket."

"Why the heck would Jackie do all this? Don't tell me she's in love with the guy. I've never seen such a floozy," Flowers growls.

Why? Why indeed?

My lips start moving before my brain catches up. "Attention. The murder was on TV. She's been angling for a promotion ever since. She's gotten national coverage outta this."

Flowers gives me a slight nod. Wait. Is that acceptance? Acknowledgement? But then he speaks, "Well, this is nice. In theory. But we don't have the ring. We don't have any proof to tie Jackie in."

"They obviously got rid of the ring." I roll my eyes. "Even a thickhead knows to get rid of the murder weapon. Mason would have tossed it somewhere. It's like murder 101."

Flowers stares me down. With his scary stare. The one that forces me into doing extra push-ups even when I feel like dying. "Prove it. Find the ring."

It takes a second. But a cheshire grin slowly spreads over my face. "To solve this case, we need to find a *lost* murder weapon?" I waggle my eyebrows.

"Yes."

"What's this?" Bennett looks between us.

"Well, it just so happens that the commander has helped me become proficient at losing things."

Bennett's jealousy flares up again. This time, I'm too giddy to do anything but fan it.

"Mr. Flores, we'll have to see if all those *hard* early-morning sessions paid off." I wink.

Flowers groans at the innuendo and holds up a hand to ward off Bennett's fury. "Not like that."

I link arms with both men, ignoring the hot rage on one side and the utter discomfort on the other. My eyes light up as I look at Seena declare, "Field trip!"

WE PILE OUT OF BENNETT'S GOVERNMENT-ISSUED SUV AND walk up the steps to Town Hall. Jordan, another recruit, is on guard duty this afternoon. He stands near the spelled salt line cordoning off the first crime scene. He's clearly on high alert, because he's got a half-eaten candy bar in his hand.

I steal the candy bar and take a bite.

"Hey!" Jordan complains.

"Good to see you too. Anybody been by?"

Jordan rolls his eyes. "Only every five minutes. Honeycutt's people really want us to solve this case so they can start making announcements and holding meetings again."

I nod. "Wish granted."

Jordan looks at Bennett, "You found the guy?"

I pat Jordan's shoulder. "Need to work on the inherent sexism."

Seena rolls his eyes at us. "Come on, Loser. Let's get this over with."

I step over the salt line, feeling the electric buzz as the line senses my badge and relaxes.

I pull my phone out of my purse. In a touch of inspiration, I turn the flashlight function on. Who says that thing is useless? Not me. Not today, anyway.

I take a deep breath, ignoring the skeptical looks from Ben and Seena.

I steady my nerves and hold out my phone. I do not think about how this could be a very expensive mistake. One last deep breath. Focus.

"I've lost my cellphone in the same location as Jackie Hanna's emerald poison ring."

The phone disappears.

I let out a breath. Part one. Okay. Hopefully I gambled right. Hopefully she and Mason didn't throw that ring into the Pacific. That would suck. I've got nine months left on my contract.

Time for part two.

I walk over to Bennett and hold out my hand. "I need your phone."

"No way. This is government-issued." He puts a hand protectively over his pocket.

"I'm not gonna lose it. I'm gonna ping my phone."

He grunts but pulls his phone out.

I take a deep breath and open the Find My Phone app. I pray he hasn't taken me off the contact list yet. I scroll through the numbers. I see mine. I let out a sigh of relief. I could ping my phone through the internet. But this is way faster. And right now, I'm desperate to see where they ditched that ring. My hands shake slightly as I punch the screen and activate the homing device.

"Alright boys. Let's spread out and search."

I knew Mason didn't have a lot of time out of everyone's line of sight. What I didn't expect was to find pinging coming from the men's restroom.

"Hey guys!" I yell. "Over here." All three come sprinting over. As if this is the most amazing and outrageous thing. Or as if it's dinnertime. Looks the same to me, anyway.

I let them do the honors and go into that putrid, urine-infested room first.

"Find it?" I call, once I've steeled myself with a final breath of fresh air.

I take a step in only to yelp and leap back. Bennett's standing in the middle of the floor with an empty trash bag in his hand. Garbage is scattered all over the floor. Along with my phone, pinging like an annoying alarm, flashlight shining like a beacon through what looks like a used condom.

I groan. Quadruple gross. "This is my karma for making fun of JR crawling all over the bathroom."

Everyone in the room stops what they're doing and stares.

"Crawling? Why?" Seena asks.

I wave them off. "Never mind."

"Do you see the ring?" Bennett asks, kicking aside some paper towels.

"No, but don't touch it if you see it. A touch was all it took for Becca to go under," Seena warns.

"Found it!" Flowers is in one of the stalls, where the trash tsunami overflowed under the stall door. He kicks it our way. It clatters across the tiles.

Seena freaks. "Don't touch it!" He jumps up and nearly climbs a sink.

"They're called boots." Flowers comes out of the stall and watches the ring settle in the middle of the floor.

The guys all crowd near to look at it. I hang back. My eyes search the bathroom. What are we gonna use to scoop that ring up? I'm not sure the poison won't leach through paper towels. Or plastic bags.

I hear a clink. And, "Yes!" in Bennett's growly voice.

Ben holds up his investigator badge. He's unpinned it and stabbed it through the ring. Now the ring rests on his five-pointed star. Like some kind of metallic pentagram of evil.

I shudder. "Alright. One item down. Now who's gonna grab my phone?"

Seena shoulders past me to hold the door open for Bennett. "Need to work on the inherent sexism, Loser. You're gonna have to get it yourself."

Damn!

S o, obvi, next stop is Jackie's place. Bennett gets warrant approval on the road and a nice little email doc on his phone complete with the judge's signature.

We discuss the second murder on the way.

"Maybe Mason got cold feet?" Seena suggests

"Maybe he still wanted to go after Gor and Jackie'd already gotten what she wanted," Bennett tosses out.

Flowers even contributes, "She was the one to find the body, and statistically—"

"Eighty-five percent of homicides end with the murderer found standing over the body," Seena and I recite together.

Bennett parks down the street and a hazmat witch shows up to collect the ring and bring it back to the lab.

Bennett and Flowers go first, guns drawn. In case.

Jackie's not at her place. I mean, what are the odds? Murderer going underground. I know. Totally shocking, right?

We bust in anyway because we have a warrant and we're gathering evidence. Good thing she lives in a tiny bungalow buried under a ton of palm trees, otherwise neighbors would be staring.

Her house is totally weird. I mean, who puts up that many photos of themselves? With no one else in them? She also has an unhealthy obsession with baby pink. She even has a pink light shining down on a little aquarium where a lizard and a frog are living in semi-harmony.

Which, when we make it to her bedroom, morphs into an unhealthy obsession with Pegasuses. Pegasi? Yeah, I do not know how to say that word. A pegasus is rare. They're kinda like the tigers of the horse shifter world. Alpha. Loners. Dangerous. Okay, maybe I can see the appeal. A little.

Anyway, her room is like some teen fangirl monstrosity. Only adulted. She doesn't have posters. She has full canvas prints of hot, muscled, half-shifted pegasi men showing off their wings and ripping their shirts off.

Seena snorts beside me as he starts shuffling through the perfume and potion bottles on Jackie's dresser.

"What? Don't like her taste? She's into horses."

"She's a murderer. And she's not into horses. She's into ego. Big egos."

"Yeah, well I bet another part of them is pretty big too," I say as I bend to check under the bed. I pull out a box and slide off the lid. It's a memory box, stuffed full of concert tickets, letters, random photos of Jackie and friends. "Oh crap." I can just imagine Flowers forcing me to go through this for the next two hours.

I consider shoving the box back under the bed but damn! It's like he's reading my mind. Flowers pops up on our side of the room.

"Good. Bring that, Fox. Got anything, Mostafavipour?"

Seena holds up a couple bottles. "She has a collection of low-level illegal potions here, I think. Need lab testing to confirm."

"Good. Extra charges the D.A. can toss on. I'll have a witch come by and check the place for spells too."

Bennett wanders up with a calendar in his hands. "So, I don't think we need to set too many guys to watch this place. It looks like there's some kind of music festival thing she's going to. Unless she suspects we're onto her." He holds up the calendar.

I squint to read, "Rainbow Cloud Wishes. Hold up." I quickly sift through the clutter in the box and grab a few items. Tickets. Brochures with a rainbow and cloud, just like the poster on McDonnelly's wall. "She's been to this before. Looks like it's a thing for her. Even got backstage passes."

"Ugh," Seena groans.

We all turn to him.

"Rainbow Cloud *Crap* is this god-awful band from L.A. They've been catching on lately. With idiots. Like Jackie. They think they're a punk-magic band. To be clear, they're not. They suck. And all these stupid girls dress up in costume for their concerts."

I flick through the photos. Jackie deleted Mason's computer pictures. But she hasn't burned hers. She must not know we're onto her yet. "Here's a photo of her and Mason at a concert." I flick through a couple more. "Looks like they were super fans."

An evil idea spreads through my mind like a thundercloud. "So ... we know where our murderer will be later tonight."

"Yeah, in a crowd of ten thousand people at an open-air concert where she can escape a million different ways," Bennett's scrolling through the concert deets on his phone.

"We'll have to wait," Flowers agrees with the boss.

"Ah, but we also know her weakness," My grin spread and glee crackles like lightning in my stomach. I stare hard at Seena. My eyes flicker between him and the posters.

"No. No! I figured out it was Mason," he sputters.

"Don't think of it as losing the bet. You didn't. Think of it as being a hero."

"I don't need to be a hero," Seena protests.

"Then why are you working here?"

Flowers and Bennett haven't caught on yet.

Flowers eyes bounce between us. "What are you arguing about?"

"Seena's gonna be our trojan horse."

"Oh, that cleared it up. Thanks, Fox." He glares down at me.

But even his glare can't dampen my joy. "Seena's gonna be our trojan *pegasus*."

The men's eyes flit to the posters on the wall.

"You think that will work?" Flowers is, as always, skeptical.

"If we call the arena and find out if she's got a backstage pass…" Bennett eyes Seena. "Only about fifty people get back there. Plus crew. Entrances and exits already guarded."

"This is a bad idea!" Seena's voice cracks a bit as he sees the guys start to sway.

"All you'd have to do is talk to her. Give us enough time to surround her."

"Yes, talking to women is my forte," Seena rolls his eyes.

"We're gonna make you look so good that she's the one who's gonna talk to you," I reassure him.

He stares daggers at me. "Bisho'ur."

I shrug. "Can't insult me if I don't know what it means."

"It means you're an idiot."

My grin just doubles. "I think you're getting confused with your languages again. You mean genius."

"I don't have wings."

His excuses are getting more pathetic by the second. "Lucky for you, I know a lady whose been sewing herself a set of wings for a wedding," I blow on my shoulder and dust it off. That's right. I'm feeling that badass at the moment.

Bennett's already got his phone out, making calls.

I lean toward Seena, who's slumped down against the dresser. "What kind of stencil do you want on your hip? Ice cream cone? Or ... I know! A rainbow and cloud! So she'll think you're a big fan too."

"I hate you."

"You are gonna be the envy of our entire class. You are gonna be the guy who caught the big City Council Killer."

"I can't believe she gave herself that name."

"Ego right?"

Seena just sighs.

Now that he's resigned to his fate, I pull out my phone and speed dial Sarah Snow. She answers on the second ring.

"Hey, it's Lyon. I'm gonna need those wings you made."

"Sorry, what's that, sugar?"

"Your wings. And all the body glitter you've got. Police business. We'll write you a check."

"Is this for that murder case?"

"Can't say."

"Ooooh! It is! Well of course, honey, whatever you need."

"We'll be there in twenty to pick them up."

As I hang up, Flowers narrows his eyes. "Are you friends with a hooker? Who has fake wings and body glitter just sitting around their house?"

I laugh. "You can go inside and pick them up for me. See for yourself."

FLOWERS LOOKS TRAUMATIZED AS HE CLIMBS INTO THE CAR, A pair of wings wrapped in plastic trailing the ground behind him.

"Get the body glitter too?" I ask.

"I can't believe I'm saying this, but I think we might have just done a public service," he swipes a hand over his eyes.

"Mrs. Snow is an amazing neighbor," I chide.

"What took so long?" Bennett pulls away from the curb and steers toward his house. He decided (graciously) not to perform Seena's makeover at the office. In front of everyone.

"She refused to hand over the wings until she'd … modeled them."

I snort. Seena guffaws.

"It's not funny. I'm pretty sure I'll never be able to look at another winged woman without flashbacks."

I bite my lip. I can't be sure, but Sarah knows what a hard time Flowers has been giving me. Was this payback? I really hope so. I'll have to ask her later, but for now, I've got a pony to dress up.

Two hours later, I can't believe my eyes. Or the secret snapshots I've taken with my phone. Seena might be prettier than me. I may have to hate him a little.

Seena shifted into a horse in the bathroom. And man, whatever muscle he's missing as a guy he makes up for as a horse. Albeit a tiny one.

We've painted him jet black. I had a Broomer deliver some rainbow stencils, paint, and a studded leather collar to Bennett's house. And then I got crafting.

The wings though. OMG. Underwear models watch out. Mrs. Snow should be making and selling these suckers instead of those nasty potions she's obsessed with. Nah. Nix that. She saved Becca—who is totally getting a copy of these photos.

I straighten the last lock of Seena's mane when Bennett calls time.

While I created art, the guys did all the legwork to get Seena approved for backstage and set up the trap. I take a step back from Seena, hands in the air like they do on those nude painting competition shows.

"Bam! Masterpiece!" I stick my hands out and showcase my work, earning myself an approving nod from Bennett, who ducks out (I think to avoid laughing in Seena's face).

Seena groans as he looks at himself in the mirror. "Ugh. I look like a frickin' female."

273

"You mean a blue-ribbon show pony. And no way you look like a female. You've got the leather thing going on. And look, I put lightning bolts through your rainbow clouds. Totally manly."

I'm working so hard not to laugh. But it's hard. This is literally the best moment of my life. "If there's a shootout tonight and I die, I think I will have achieved my life's goal. Which I didn't even know until this very moment is seeing you dressed like this."

"You know revenge is a bitch, right?"

"I look forward to meeting her." I'm pretty sure he can't do anything to top this. If he can … well good on him.

Seena gives me a hard look but doesn't have any more time before the guys trot him out to a horse trailer and load him up for the concert.

I toss an extra vial of glitter into my pocket in case Seena needs touch ups when we get there.

Flowers sidles up to me as we watch Bennett drive off with our magnificent murderer-catching lure. "You know, Fox. If this works, it might be the second time in your life you had a decent idea."

"Decent? I'm probably gonna make posters out of the photos I took in the bathroom."

"If you do, I might know someone who wants one."

I turn to stare. Flowers has the hint of a smirk on his face.

"Come on, you gotta admit, that's the funniest forkin' thing you've ever seen."

Of course, that ruins it. Because I'm not allowed to tell Flowers to admit anything. Ever.

The smirk disappears. His eyes turn cold. "Get your mind back in the game, rookie."

He turns on his heel and I'm forced to follow. Because he and I will be holed up for hours in a music equipment trailer waiting for the 'backstage experience' after this concert. Peachy. Just what I want. To sit in the dark crammed in next to a grumpy tiger shifter.

I pull out my phone as Flores climbs onto his motorcycle. Because, of course, he's too manly to drive in a car. He has to feel the motor vibrate his balls. He tosses me the helmet, which I miss.

"Dammit, Fox!"

"Sorry. It was the helmet or my phone."

"You don't need your phone."

"I do if I'm gonna survive you," I scoop up the helmet and press send on the phone.

"What the hell's that supposed to mean?" Flores grumbles as I reluctantly climb on behind him.

"I ordered food. So you won't be the most grumptastic person on the planet." I don't tell him that I spent forty of my last sixty gold on frickin' meat. Because then he'd refuse it. But, denting my bank account is better than the dent my head's likely to get otherwise.

"We're supposed to be hidden," he growls, as he starts the motorcycle.

"We will be. But it's called a steak-out right?" I laugh at my own joke as I strap on the helmet and climb uncomfortably on behind him. I wrap my hands around his torso and I can feel his pecs through his jacket. That shouldn't be possible, right?

"Not funny," he shakes his head.

"I'm hilarious."

"You're an annoying loudmouth," he shoots back. Then he hits the gas and anything else I might say is ripped away by the wind.

It's time to catch a baddie.

## 22

Flowers and I eat and then take turns peering through a gap between the doors of the equipment trailer.

The waiting game sucks. Particularly when the person you're waiting with doesn't want to play any games whatsoever.

My ideas for charades, scary-stories, and crazy sound-effects are all shot down.

Flower's ideas for fun waiting activities are squats, wall-sits, calf raises. In short, torture. And he likes his torture with a side of silence. (Relative silence since the opening act is screeching onstage.)

After a while, I can't help myself. The silence is driving me nuts.

"How's your family?"

"What?"

"Got a mom? Sisters? Brothers?"

"I don't talk about personal shit."

"You know now I'm gonna take that as a personal challenge to find out, right?"

"They're called boundaries, Lyon. Get some." His tone is harsh.

"What's that supposed to mean?"

"Stop running around screwing with the boss's head. Focus on work at work."

"I'm not—"

"Horse shit. You're pathetic. Trying to get ahead."

"I'm not. We dated years ago—"

"Liar."

"I'm not. We hooked up before I got this job—"

"I don't want or need any details." Flowers turns away and peers through the crack again.

"I wasn't gonna give them to you. We aren't together because I told him—"

"Can't follow a single direction. No details."

"We aren't together!" I snarl.

Flowers holds up a fist. At first, I'm ready to smack it down, thinking he's shushing me. But then he turns his head and widens the crack a bit.

"I think she took the bait."

"What?" I'm next to him in two seconds, spat forgotten. I'm shoving close, trying to see. He won't budge. Because he's that kind of jerk. Fine. I get on my knees and shove his legs aside so I can peer outside. I'm not above acting like I'm three.

Jackie Hanna, in a tutu and rainbow-striped pigtails, is talking to Seena, petting his wings and giggling like a maniac.

"Ha! Parlor, fly. Welcome."

"What?" Flowers is staring down at me like I'm some kind of freak.

"I'm the spider."

He raises an eyebrow.

"Nothing. Never mind. My grandma's old saying. Welcome to my parlor said the spider to the—"

The radio in my ear buzzes to life and I cut myself off before Flowers shoves a palm in my face to make me shut up.

Bennett's voice crackles with static. "Start closing in."

Flowers bounds out of the trailer like it's on fire, leaving me to amble out behind and shut the doors so they don't swing free and make a racket.

Unfortunately, Jackie's not a reporter for nothing. Her sharp eyes notice Flowers subtly running at her like a damn football player.

Suddenly, Seena's on the ground. He hits his hidden chest mic with his snout, screaming, "She's got a gun! Invisible silent fucking gun!" He nuzzles his thigh. Flowers stops to help him and Jackie changes direction.

"Shnikes!" I hit the mic and let the team know she's headed west.

I turn on the speed. I focus on Jackie. Only Jackie. On those ridiculous pig tails. On her blue glitter top. She raises a hand.

I duck. I don't hear a bullet, but it must whizz right over my head. I glance back. Behind me, a drum bursts apart. Shit!

When I turn back I realize … we're now backstage. And where's she running? Yeah, you guessed it. Center stage.

Well, if she wants to get arrested in front of a crowd of thousands … so be it. I charge after her.

Jackie bolts for the edge of the stage and just dives.

"Fudge nuggets!"

Jackie surfaces, and she's surfing the crowd. They're eagerly carrying her away from me.

The band onstage has stopped playing. They're staring at me, owl shifters who've let their eyes shift into bright glowing orbs for the show. Security's closing in, ready to throw me off the stage like some groupie. I don't see Flowers. Bennett's yelling orders in my ear, but the static is so loud I can't understand him. What do I do?

I run to the singer and grab his mic. He just stares at me through stringy emo hair.

Moment of truth. Do I tell these people I'm a cop in training and she's a killer? Visions of mass panic, screaming, and trampling enter my brain. Nope. Nope. Come on stupid me. Think. What would make me wanna help someone out?

I yell into the mic. "My sister just hooked up with my boyfriend. Stop that witch!"

Bam. Mic drop. Literally. I toss it down onstage.

I see Jackie disappear from the surface of the crowd. I run to the edge of the stage and jump onto the willing hands of a dozen men wearing Rainbow Cloud shirts.

I hear a chorus of "Get her."

"She deserves what's coming!"

"Give it to her!"

It was a gamble, but shifters hate cheating. Betraying the pack. Obvi, there are other magical creatures here, but thank you Flowers for the remedial lessons. Shifters love loyalty. And with a shifter band onstage, I figured the percentage of the crowd would be higher. I think I gambled right.

I know I did when the crowd sets me down right in front of Jackie and then forms a tight circle around us. A fight circle.

Crap. I can't fight a woman with an invisible gun! She could kill me. She could kill people behind me. And it would be all my fault.

Heat floods my body. That thought is a nightmare. *Nobody* can die because of me. I can't let that happen. I've gotta get her to lose the weapon!

I almost smack myself in the forehead. As Jackie whirls toward me, I mutter, "Jackie Hanna's lost her gun."

She raises her hand. I feel a bullet whiz by my left thigh.

Fuck!

I try to ignore the crowd. Zero my focus. I picture Luke. "That bullet's lost in the ground."

My right leg starts to tingle. Then burn, just like it did when I practiced. I don't hear screams behind me. Please don't let anyone be shot.

I dunno if that worked, but I have to try again. I watch Jackie's fingers reach for the trigger a second time. It feels like she's moving in slow motion as I speak. "Jackie's lost her gun in Diego Flores' office."

Jackie raises her hand. I clench my eyes shut. Please work. Please *please* have worked.

*Smack!*

She smashes my face with her hand.

I breathe a sigh of relief. Until she punches me again. Right in the eye.

"Trucking witch!" I shove her back and I hit the radio button in my ear and turn on my work mic. "We're in the crowd. There's a fight circle around us." Jackie's eyes narrow. I can tell she's figured out I'm a cop.

I pull out handcuffs, the only police-issued item I'm allowed to have, since I'm still in training.

Jackie's lips move. And then she disappears.

Godmother freaking dammit! Why does a nymph have better magic than me?

Without warning, my hair screams in pain. My face is yanked down. Into an invisible knee. I taste blood.

Are you shitting me? I have to fight an invisible suspect? She yanks my hair to the side and *pow*—my ear's ringing.

The crowd around us boos and hisses.

I wildly toss punches. I latch onto skin and pinch somewhere hard enough to make her yowl.

But she's beating me. My head's getting woozy.

I need to be able to see her. The thought flashes like bright neon in my brain. That, or I'm seeing colors from all the punches.

I reach into my pocket and grab that vial of glitter I saved. Better than nothing. I fling it at her.

*Whoosh.*

Suddenly we're in the air. Then I'm not. She drops me.

I hit the ground hard. I stand up quick. What happened? Did I lose her?

I glance up. She's not invisible anymore. Flying up must have shocked her system enough to disrupt her invisibility spell.

Jackie's boobs are covered in gold glittering ... pixie dust. They're bobbing in the air like balloons, hitting her in the chin. She tries to shove them down but can't. They bobble back to smack her face. She growls.

I giggle.

She kicks out at me, but that just flips her backward. Her boobs are dangerously close to bobbing out of her top.

She's stuck there. Suspended. As a nymph, she can't fly. Can't move beyond the basic lift the dust gives her.

I reach for my camera phone. "You like photos of yourself right, Jackie?"

Flowers and Bennett come barreling through the edge of the circle as I take a photo with full flash.

"What happened?" Flowers asks.

I shrug, slipping the vial of pixie dust back into my pocket. No need for Tabby and Mrs. Snow to get in trouble after all the help they've given us.

"Someone in the crowd was trying to help me out."

Flowers narrows his eyes.

"What about all the feathers?"

That's when I notice the ground near me is littered with feathers.

I shrug. "Maybe someone in the crowd wore a boa?"

Ben turns to Jackie and slips his cuffs over her floating wrists. "You're under arrest, for the murders of Bernard Bell and Mason McDonnelly." The fight circle buzzes with this new tidbit. Phones start flashing as people take pictures.

Flowers heads off through the crush of people, creating a path.

Ben tries to pull Jackie down, but the pixie dust is too strong. So, he hooks his hand over the chain in her cuffs and leads her away through the crowd, like a big dumb parade float.

## 23

"**S**how me again!" Becca demands, a naughty twinkle sparkling in her eyes that I'm pretty sure matches the one in mine.

I'm sitting on the side of her hospital bed, swiping through photos on my phone.

In the stall next door, Seena groans. "No! You've already seen them four times." He's still a horse (though not as pretty since he's washed off his glam makeup). The docs say he needs to stay shifted until he heals. Couple more hours. They did magic up a stall next to Becca though, which he thought was nice. Until I showed up with photo-sabotage.

We've been laughing for half an hour.

"Please—" Seena starts.

"Shut up, boyfriend," Becca retorts.

Seena's head pops through the stall. He blows his bangs out of his eyes. "You mean it?"

She grins. "How could I turn down such a pretty face? Yeah. You can take me to dinner once you're all better."

He paws the ground, and winces.

"Calm down, big boy. You need to save your strength so we can play rodeo later," Becca winks.

I cover my ears. "Ahhh! They're burning!"

She gives me an apologetic shrug. I stand and slide over the box of cookies I brought her.

"You aren't leaving?" she tosses out a pouty lip.

"Gotta get to a wedding," I shrug.

"Ooh! I want pics of that too!" Becca squeals.

"Not so sure you do. The bride's supposedly a monster."

"For real? What kind? Gorgon? Chupacabra?"

"Nope. A nymph with a monster on the inside."

"Gotcha. Well, thanks again for catching Jackie. Did Bennett ever text you back to say if she confessed?"

I pull out my phone as I head toward the door. "Nope. Not yet. Might still be questioning her."

"She'll confess," Seena sounds sure of himself. "I suggested they put a camera in the room and tell her it was a live stream. She won't be able to resist."

I stick my hand in his stall and give his nose a pet. "Nice work, partner."

"Did you a pick a date for the dance, Loser?"

I laugh. "I don't tend to torture my dates. So, no. Tonight I'm stag."

"And tomorrow?"

I glide out the door. "Bye, Seena!"

The Broomer drops me off at my apartment so I can get dressed. I toss on a pale blue midi dress with a low neckline and I'm finishing my makeup when there's a knock at the door.

Bennett's broad shoulders nearly span the door frame.

"Hey!"

"Hey," his eyes sweep down my figure and harden. "Date?" The word comes out strangled.

"Nope. Going to a nightmare wedding to support JR."

"JR's getting married?"

"JR's a bridesmaid for a demon."

"What level?"

I sigh. I really need to just tell everyone Camila's a shrew. "Not a demon-demon. A woman with no soul, who bosses around JR, changes wedding plans on a dime, and essentially should be banished to the depths of hell. Instead, she's moving to Jersey with the new hubby."

"Basically equivalent."

I shrug. "So, what's up? Jackie confess?"

"Yup. Asked for makeup to touch her face up and gave a full confession to the camera."

I offer him a high five. "Nice work, boss."

He doesn't hit my hand. He looks at it like it hurts. "Is that what we are now? Am I just your boss?"

I bite my lip. I wasn't ready for this confrontation. But it's here. He's pushing it again. "I've already told you twenty times, I need space."

"But you're dating Luke."

"I went on one date."

"But if he asks …"

I stare up at Bennett. And here's my problem. "You aren't giving me space Bennett." He opens his mouth to argue. I hold up a hand to stop him. "You can do it for a couple days, sure. But then you come back and bug me. And make it uncomfortable. Make people like Flowers think I'm using you to get ahead."

"I can't stand it for more than a few days because I love you, Lyon!" He hits the doorjamb.

That just pisses me off. "Yeah, well I had to stand it for two years while you went and fought your clan and did whatever you needed to do. And I didn't even get the courtesy of knowing you cared."

"It's not the same."

"And there it is. You don't respect that this is important to me."

"I do! I helped you prove yourself on this case. This is the second killer you've caught, Ly. And God, when you're on fire, linking up the evidence, it's so hot. I don't know how you expect me to control myself."

I don't respond immediately, and Bennett's tone gets hesitant. "You do think it's hot, right?"

I shake my head. "You're missing the point." I grab my purse from the side table. I take out my keys. "I have to go."

Bennett steps back onto the landing. "So, that's it?"

"If you can't give me what I want, that's it." I lock my door and march to the stairs.

"So you're dating the vampire?"

"Yup."

I hear the rip of clothing behind me. I turn on the stairs just as Bennett launches his dragon form into the sky. My heart lurches. But my head stands firm. I don't want to hurt him. But I do care about my own integrity. Jacob said I needed a cheerleader. But I don't just want someone who cheers me on when I'm clever. I want someone who cheers me on when I've decided to do something crazy. Something hard. Because I think it's good for me. Because I think it's what's right.

I run back up and collect Ben's torn clothes—wouldn't look good for an investigator to get in trouble for public shifting. I toss them in the trash.

Getting drunk sounds good right now. So, I head to the wedding.

THE OAKS IS A SPRAWLING ESTATE RUN BY DRYADS. CAMILA'S wedding is in the largest ballroom. Lush moss covers the ground. Marble columns reach thirty feet into the air to hold up a glass ceiling. Purple clematis and wisteria adorn the walls and make the room smell of summer, even though outside the trees are losing leaves. Orbs of yellow light and floating candelabras cast a soft glow on the room. The paper cranes weave throughout the room. Overall, the effect is beautiful, just slightly marred by the occasional crane going kamikaze into a candle.

"Lyon!" Mrs. Snow is resplendent in a white suit encrusted with rhinestones, a pattern matched by the mini-wings she wears on her back. She hugs me.

"Made yourself a new set? They look nice."

She grins. "A little last minute, but I do think they turned out pretty nice—oh my lord, do you see that girl?" Mrs. Snow nods toward a woman clad in a form-fitting silk suit. "Her pants are so tight I can see her religion!"

I choke. I die. I grab the goblin next to me and laugh in his face. Oh, Mrs. Snow! She has no idea what a godsend she is.

When I'm back in control, I ask her, "Where's Tabby?"

"Didn't you see?" Mrs. Snow nods to a row of benches at the front of the room. I squint. And then my eyes go as wide as saucers. Tabby's on the front bench, the one reserved for family. And she's not in human form. She's a cat. Sitting right next to her? Max the Cat.

"Camila forgave JR just about anything when she saw JR brought a City Councilor to her wedding," Mrs. Snow confides.

"How is JR?"

Before she gets a chance to answer, a satyr pan-flute group starts to play. We have to take our seats.

The wedding is … just like every other wedding. Vows and wet eyes and a cheer at the kiss. I don't know why Camila's spent so much on it when it's the same as every other wedding I've ever been to … until they serve the food. Mmm. I wish I'd brought a bigger purse.

After three drinks, even JR is starting to enjoy herself. We head out to the dance floor and I'm sorry to say, Sarah Snow puts us all to shame.

I FLIT UP THE STAIRS TO MY HOUSE, TIPSY AND SEMI-contented. I still feel bad about Bennett. But after the drunken reassurances of Tabby, Sarah Snow, JR (and even a drunken Max the Cat shouting, "Girl, you need to tap that vamp ass!") I kinda feel like I made the right choice.

I unlock the door, super glad drunk me didn't slip into old habits and lose my keys.

I'm barely inside before my phone buzzes.

*I miss you.*

I have to double check the sender. Yes, I'm that drunk. It's from Luke.

*Miss you too.*

*I got something for you.*

*Yeah? What is it?*

*You'll have to wait and find out.*

I groan.

*I want it now.*

Just then, there's a knock at my door. I skip (okay, fine, I trip) over to the door, ecstatic. I pull it open.

But it's not Luke. It's a delivery man. He stares boredly at me. "Lyon Fox?"

"Yup."

"These are for you," he hands over a white bakery box. OMG. Luke, keys to my heart. Keys to my heart. I bring them to the kitchen counter and open the box.

Two dozen frosted heart cookies are nestled in wax paper, alternating pink and red. My eyes blur. I swipe at them.

I grab a cookie. And scream.

I drop it.

Because as soon as I touched the cookie, a symbol appeared on top of the frosting. A black tombstone surrounded by a circle.

The symbol of the Crypts.

Read Book 3 Now!

## PREVIEW OF BOOK 3 - WHAT THE FAE

A sixth sense jerks me awake. My heart pounds and I lash out, my arm swinging wildly. My fist connects with something—someone.

"Motherfucker!"

"JR?" Crap. She never curses. I must have hit her hard. I sit up and my head sways unsteadily. (Heads do that after you've tried to drink away your guy problems.)

JR plops down on the bed beside me, still in her bridesmaid dress from last night, a dress that showcases her curves. My eyes adjust to the afternoon light. She's cradling her face. Poor nymph's gonna have a shiner.

"Best friends have to forgive each other for at least one face punch, right?"

She turns toward me, the skin by her eye already swelling like a goose egg. "I don't think that's a thing."

"Definitely a thing!" her boyfriend, Danny Lovato, calls from my living room.

I grin. "I'm glad he's good for something."

"I'm good for a lotta things. You just aren't privy to most of them," Danny saunters into the room on his hooves and hands JR an ice pack.

Damn thoughtful satyr boyfriends.

Damn boyfriends in general.

Damn my taste in boyfriends.

JR groans and shoves the icepack on her face. Danny shoves something into his mouth.

I do a double take, then launch myself across the bed. "No!"

I latch onto Danny and grab the cookie out of his hand. We fall to the floor.

"Spit it out!"

"Learn to share!"

"I'm serious. Spit it out." I hold up the cookie. A heart-shaped sugar cookie, it now has a bite missing. But in the middle of the pink icing is the Crypts' symbol. When Danny touched the cookie, a tombstone inside a circle appeared. The sign of the most dangerous vampire gang in town.

"What the hell?" Danny spits his bite out. Finally.

"What is that?" JR asks.

"This is why I called you. I don't know what to do." I toss her the cookie to examine, then sink my face into my hands. "Luke sent them."

"That vamp you're dating?" Danny asks.

"He sent you cookies with the Crypts' gang sign on them?" JR turns the cookie upside down, as if something else might appear.

I nod. Tears form in my eyes. I'm not sure why he sent them. Or what it means. But it can't be good. The cookies scared the crap outta me. And I don't know why he'd do that. We just started dating. Why would he want to scare me?

"That ass—" JR is about to rip Luke a new one. I can see it in her eyes. The brown turns tawny when she's pissed.

Danny's gagging stops her.

We both turn to look at him. His face is swollen to twice its normal size. He grabs at his throat. His eyes bulge.

Tingles prick my body as I realize those cookies weren't just meant to scare me. "Crud! We have to get him to the hospital!" I trip over him in my haste to get to my phone. I shove my blonde hair out of my eyes, grab my cell off the nightstand, and dial 666.

"Tres Lunas Emergency Services."

"I think my friend was poisoned."

"Species?"

"He's a satyr. Half man-half goat."

"Permission to do a locating spell on you?"

"Yes!" I yell.

Danny's starting to turn blue.

JR sobs.

Eff no. This can't be happening. She just caught the bouquet at her cousin's wedding last night!

"Location spell started. Emergency team is on the way. Can you describe your situation for me? What kind of poison?"

I'm shaking. Hard. Like a branch in a hurricane. "I dunno. Poisoned cookie."

"Food poisoning?"

"The cookie shows a Crypts' symbol. So, no. I don't think it's just food poisoning," my voice cracks.

The operator gasps.

"We're going to route you to the city hospital via teleportation. It will be fastest. How many people, so I can tell the Emergency Response Wizard?"

"Three." I hang up the phone as there's a knock on the door. "They're here."

I'm not sure JR even hears me. She's cradling Danny's head and rocking back and forth.

I stumble to the door, still a little drunk, definitely a bit shaky, and open it for a wizard dressed in white.

"Emergency—"

"This way." I shove him inside, lock the front door, and drag him to my bedroom.

Three seconds later, JR, Danny, and I are in a hospital waiting room.

And that's when I realize, I'm in my underwear.

An elf doctor comes out and starts talking to JR, who somehow remembered to bring the cookie with her.

He sends it to the lab for testing.

He sends Danny somewhere to get his stomach pumped and spelled.

He sends me to the bathroom to put on his spare sweater and some hospital socks.

I avoid looking in the mirror. I don't want to see my blonde bed-head, or the raccoon eyes from my blue eyeliner from last night. I just change as quickly as I can and duck out of the restroom.

That's how I end up wandering the hall, in nothing but an orange, button-up argyle sweater and lime green—don't steal us we're hospital property—socks.

I'm sure I look crazy. Or like a homeless jester.

Which is exactly the look you want to go for when you run into your ex.

Bennett comes striding out of a patient's room with an air of authority. He's in his cop uniform and, of course, the sleeves are molded to his biceps. With his sleek black hair and green eyes, he looks like a walking calendar model. Dammit!

When he sees me, he stops—just straight up freezes.

And that's when the dam breaks.

"Lyon, what are you doing here?"

"Danny's here. It's all my fault."

"Danny?"

"JR's boyfriend. I punched her."

"What?"

"I was sleeping. I didn't know it was her."

"You aren't making any sense."

I slide down the wall. "I know. Okay. Luke sent me cookies."

Bennett's jaw clenches. "And?"

I laugh bitterly as I wipe off some tears, "And they're poisoned. And they have a Crypts' symbol on them."

Bennett squats and grabs my shoulder. "Are you serious?"

His touch is warm, and gentle. And his face shows only concern. It soothes me and I'm able to stop the flood. I need to get back in control. Whatever Luke's done, this is big. Whatever he meant, this is serious. Danny's hurt. And I need Bennett's help. I swallow and nod.

I try to explain. But I'm still a little drunk, "Danny bit a cookie. And they're pumping him. Back there. Some elf guy is pumping him." I wave an arm in the general direction they took Danny.

Bennett runs a hand over his face. "Okay. Where are the cookies?"

"My place."

Bennett grabs his phone but leaves one hand on my shoulder. He dials. The voice that answers is not a voice I want to hear.

"Flores. Gonna send you my location. Get over here. We've got a murder and poisoning ... separate. And ... bring some extra clothes."

Bennett clicks off. He guides me down the hall until we see JR. She looks haunted. The bruise by her eye is awful. Her mascara trails down her cheeks with her tears. Her lipstick's gone. And her lips are open in that dull, vacant expression of shock I've seen on crime victims at our office.

I grab her hand.

Bennett leads us both to the cafeteria and settles us at a table.

"Stay here. I'll send Flores as soon as I can."

I rub JR's back. I try and whisper soothing things. But there's only so many times you can say, "I'm sorry," or "He'll be alright," without sounding fake.

She just stares at the wall. I wouldn't want to look at me either.

Do best friends have to forgive each other for accidentally poisoning a boyfriend? I don't think so.

If I hadn't gotten drunk and called JR, this wouldn't have happened.

If I'd thrown away those cookies, this wouldn't have happened.

If I hadn't encouraged Luke, this wouldn't have happened.

I'm about to spiral into wicked self-pity. Which I don't deserve. JR deserves all the pity. So, I stand, determined to at least be useful.

I get in line and order some coffee and breakfast bars. The D team must be working the hospital cafeteria—do they even have an A team at a hospital cafeteria?—because it takes forever for the cyclops behind the counter to come back with a pair of pre-packaged bars.

"Better check the expiration date," the man behind me in line says.

"Good call." I look. Ah, yeah, these are like two years expired. I slide the bars back across the counter.

"Never mind on these. Just the coffee."

The cafeteria cyclops glares at me.

"Three gold."

Crap! I forgot my wallet. All I have is my phone. I peer behind me. JR doesn't have hers either.

"Umm ... we kinda teleported here for an emergency. Do you have like a credit—"

"I got it." The man behind me leans forward and tosses five gold coins on the counter. "I'll take a coffee too, Mick."

I finally turn and fully face him. He's mid-forties. His face looks like the surface of the moon. Bet his high school years sucked. But his eyes have laugh lines. So hopefully it all worked out for him. In any case, he turned out nice enough to buy a half-clothed woman a drink. A non-alcoholic drink.

I hold out a hand. "Thank you. I'm Lyon Fox, by the way."

"Bruce Parker." He shakes my hand with a firm grip and then points toward the sapphire embedded in my chin.

"You fae?"

I roll my eyes. "Barely. And not by choice."

He laughs and grabs his coffee. "I know what you mean." He gestures to an onyx stone embedded near his left temple. It could pass for a nasty mole if the light didn't catch it right.

We head to the condiments table for creamer and sugar. He puts in almost as much sugar as I do.

"Man with good taste."

He shrugs. "Don't like this stuff. But working two jobs … gotta do what you gotta do. California's expensive."

"What do you do here?"

"Janitorial services."

I nod. "Been doing a lot of that myself lately."

He raises his brows. "Really?"

"I suck at magic. And my boss sees fit to punish me for it."

Bruce shakes his head.

He opens his mouth to say more but Diego Flores walks in.

A senior investigator, and my instructor at the Tres Lunas Police and Investigation Academy, Flores hates his nickname: Flowers. Because it's not serious. And Mr. Muscles is all about serious.

Flowers barks, "Fox!"

"Gotta go. Thanks for the joe." I fist bump Bruce Parker before I drop off JR's coffee.

Flowers rolls his eyes when he sees me. "Of course, *you're* the one I have to bring clothes for. Can you ever be appropriate? Just once?" He eyes my outfit and shakes his head.

"There was an emergency."

"Just get dressed." He tosses a duffel bag my way.

"JR, meet Flowers," I use his nickname just to piss him off.

Flowers nods to her and pulls out his notepad. "Ma'am. Commander French told me I should take your statement about what happened tonight."

"My best friend poisoned my boyfriend. You mean that statement?"

Flowers isn't the only one pissed at me.

Awesome. This day is killer.

Hopefully, not literally.

What the Fae: Fae'd Up and Frustrated Book 3 is available now!

# A PERSONAL NOTE FROM LYON FOX

Hey!

Whoa! That was crazy, right?

What the heck is going on? Why did Luke send me those cookies? Help me out here people. I'm freaking out. I need like Facebook photos of kittens and stuff so I can calm down. Friend Ann Denton and send them on over. Stat.

I seriously have never been so upset in my whole life. What am I going to do? Read book 3 and figure out what Luke was up to? Whoa! Hold up, Sparky! You think my author's gonna let me off the hook without asking you for reviews of this book first? Ha. Yeah right.

I mean. Come on. The Jackie boob thing was hilarious. Am I right? Boob balloons. Isn't that worth like a twenty-word book review?

Help a character out. I'd like to have the author write my books and *only* my books. Do you know how boring it is when you're just waiting for the hard-drive to be opened back up? Totes dull. Don't condemn me to the back-burner.

Hearts—

Ly

# AFTERWORD

Thank you so much for reading! You are amazing, and you are the reason I can keep dreaming up beautiful worlds. If you liked this book, please leave a review and tell your friends!

Your reviews and recommendations keep me pumped up as I write the next book. So, thanks!

# ACKNOWLEDGMENTS

Big thanks to the following people:

The hub. Obviously. For being awesome and pushing me to pursue this dream.

Raven, Ivy, Mia, Aubry, S, Janie, Christine, Rebecca, Lacey, Josephine, Misti, Kezi, and everyone else who provided feedback or love to Lyon. I couldn't have done it without you.

The kiddos. Thanks for the nights you went to sleep early.

# OTHER BOOKS BY THE AUTHOR

If you'd like to read my other work, which is more naughty and less "fade to black", but with plenty of witty banter, then feel free to read any of the following series under my other pen name - Ann Denton.

Choose from books on the following pages based on your current reading mood.

The standalone or the first book in each series are listed by mood. The darkest reads appear first and grow progressively more light-hearted so it makes it easy to find just what you're looking for next. I also tried to add some basic mood info at the bottom of each series page for you.

### FERAL PRINCESS SERIES
(Completed Trilogy)

A hot, dark shifter omegaverse with dub con, a steamy alpha, a loving beta, and a sassy omega who thought she was going to be an alpha female. She was sooo wrong, but when she's claimed by the pack alpha, make no mistake, she has something to say about it.

*Defiant - Book 1*

*Mood - #DARK #DIRTY #ALPHA*

**STALKED AND PLUCKED SERIES**
(Series of Standalones)

A fast-burn, contemporary MF romance series with very morally gray men who stalk their ladies before claiming them. The series follows a group of college girls who are best friends.

*Chaining Daisy - Book 1*

*Mood - #HOT #HOLYHELL #NEWKINKUNLOCKED*

**PINNACLE SERIES**
(Completed Duet)

A medium-burn paranormal romance about a girl who gets herself sent to a reform academy on purpose, so she can recruit criminally-minded guys to pull off the magical heist of the century. (Reverse Harem)

*Magical Academy for Delinquents #MAD - Book 1*

*Mood - #BADASS #FUN #SEXY GAMES*

### TANGLED CROWNS SERIES
(Completed Trilogy and spinoff in progress)

A medium-burn, medieval fantasy romance with a reluctant princess, the knights she jilted at the alter, and an enemies to lovers story that weaves laughter and tears together along with a plot to save the kingdom. (Reverse Harem)

*Knightfall - Book 1*

*Mood - #BANTER #REDEMPTION #WHAATJUSTHAPPENED*

**LOTTO LOVE SERIES**
(Completed Duet)

A medium-burn, contemporary romantic comedy reverse harem about winning the lotto and doing whatever the hell you want with it, even if that means holding a Bachelorette-style competition for an entire harem of hotties.

*Lotto Men - Book 1*

*Mood- #LOL #BLUSHING #NO WAY*

### RUBY - JEWELS CAFE SERIES
(Standalone)

A medium-burn, fated mates reverse harem with an angel on her last strike, some nerds and a tech demon determined to help her, and Christmas miracles.

*Ruby*

*Mood - #SWEET #AWWW #GIGGLES*

**DARK TEMPTATIONS SERIES**
(Incomplete)

A fast-burn monster reverse harem in an alternate reality where monsters rule the earth. A human woman is captured and auctioned off to the Four Terrors who will haunt her nightmares and her dreams alike.
Cowrite with Katie May.

*Ravaged by Monsters - Book 1*

*Mood - #DARK #FATED LOVE #WILD SEXY TIMES*

**BROKEN HOWL**

(Standalone)

A female omega rejects her mates so she can escape her abuser. She's sent to an island for rejects but her mates refuse to let her go…

Cowrite with Katie May.

*Broken Howl*

*Mood - #CRYING #HEALING #FIGHTING*

**DARKEST QUEEN SERIES**
(Incomplete)

The devil is a woman. And this is the story about she fell from Heaven only to rise as God's greatest enemy… (A reverse harem spinoff of the Darkest Flames series) Cowrite with Katie May.

*For Whom the Bell Tolls - Book 1*

*Mood - #FURY #SOUL-DEEP CONNECTIONS #BATTLE OF WILLS*

## DARKEST FLAMES SERIES
(Completed Trilogy with a novella)

A medium-burn paranormal romance about a girl who tries a love spell on the hot guy at school and accidentally summons demons instead. It contains psychotic, alpha males, and student/teacher relationships. (Reverse Harem) Cowrite with Katie May.

*Demon Kissed - Book 1*

*Mood - #OOPS #NAUGHTY LAUGHTER #FORBIDDEN HEAT*

### DEMON'S JOY
(Standalone)

Santa's daughter has to save Christmas from demons! And all she's got to help her are five funny reindeer. (A reverse harem spinoff of the Darkest Flames series) Cowrite with Katie May.

*Demon's Joy*

*Mood - #SILLY #HOLIDAY CHEER #YUM*

**MAGE SHIFTER WAR SERIES**
(Completed Duet)

A medium-burn paranormal mafia romance. A fae princess is taken captive by three shifter criminals. (Reverse Harem) Cowritten with Elle Middaugh.

*Fae Captive - Book 1*

*Mood - #BONNIE&CLYDE #BADASS #HOT*

**HAMMER TIME**
(Standalone)

A medium-burn paranormal comedy featuring Thor's daughter and a quest to save demigods from prison. Expect lots of ancient deities and potty humor. (Reverse Harem) Cowritten with M.J. Marstens.

*Hammer Time*

*Mood- #PUNTASTIC #NOYOUDIDN'T #SNORT*

# CONNECT AND GET SNEAK PEEKS

If you like to read exclusive snippets from different characters, make predictions with other readers, see my inspiration for books, or just come hang and be yourself, I have a Facebook reader group.

Go Here to Join Anna Dare's Reader Group:

https://www.facebook.com/AuthorAnnaDare

# ABOUT ME

I'm a Virgo. I've driven around town finding landmarks based on a friend's dream. And, I'm addicted to dark chocolate bars with espresso. I have a hubster who encourages my crazy pants ways. I have two amazing little humans who look up to me right now, but won't for long because I'm very short.

I love the arts: painting, theatre, and reading. I have an undergrad degree in Playwriting and a grad degree in Theatre History. Socrates rocks my socks.

I'm an INTJ. If you've never taken a Meyers Briggs personality test, I recommend them.

I would love to talk to you about the book. Yes you. You can ask me questions on Facebook. If you sign up for my newsletter at the link below, I'll email you about upcoming books.

www.ingramcontent.com/pod-product-compliance
Lightning Source LLC
Chambersburg PA
CBHW051331250626
47155CB00007B/2549